THE MAN FROM THE SEA

THE MAN FROM THE SEA

by

MICHAEL INNES

LONDON
VICTOR GOLLANCZ LTD
1984

First published in Great Britain February 1955
by Victor Gollancz Ltd,
14 Henrietta Street, London WC2E 8QJ
Second impression March 1955
Reissued March 1970
This edition published 1984

British Library Cataloguing in Publication Data

Innes, Michael
  The man from the sea.
  I. Title
  823'.912[F]   PR6037.T466

  ISBN 0-575-03554-4

*Printed in Great Britain by
St Edmundsbury Press, Bury St Edmunds, Suffolk*

CHAPTER I

THE BEGINNING of Cranston's adventure—the real adventure, not the intrigue—seemed as sudden and grotesque as a queer twist in a dream. The night was very still, and the empty sea as it rose and fell gently under a great low moon sighed like a woman half-awake—sighed and then stretched out cold fingers of surf to the young man's naked body sprawled on the cold sand. He told himself that he wanted to be very cold; that this was why he lingered. Lady Blair—for in his own mind he still involuntarily called her that—had disappeared among the rocks, so the hide-and-seek which was now prescriptively the next phase of the affair was due to begin. She had a childish love of it, and part of the two nocturnal hours they could risk together went regularly to a sort of ritual enactment of the game. To-night these hours were already running out. But Cranston still lingered. Prompted to give himself a reason, he recalled—conscientiously and from all the luxury of his large new knowledge—that to start with chilled limbs was additional fun. Lingering still, he turned over on his belly in the last feeble ripple of a wave. But the movement plucked obscurely and disturbingly at his mind, edging towards the light a very different reason for delay. And at that moment the thing happened.

What had appeared to be a clot of seaweed floating in with the tide became the head of a swimmer. The swimmer dropped his feet to the sea-bed and started to wade ashore. He was stripped except for a belt about his middle and a wisp of fabric round his loins. Under the sudden unnatural weight of a body long supported in

5

water, and with the staggering movement of a clumsily constructed ambulatory toy, he lurched forward foot by foot. Seeing that he was exhausted—that he might fall on his still streaming face at any moment and drown in eighteen inches of water—Cranston scrambled up and ran towards him. The man from the sea stopped dead. It was a reaction which for some reason made Cranston stop too. On this unfrequented strip of Scottish coast in the small hours, the two confronted each other like wary savages. And then the man from the sea turned his head—turned it in the direction from which he had come. He was listening.

What the man from the sea had heard Cranston caught a moment later. It was the throb of an engine. Already that night he had heard something of the sort. Lady Blair—Caryl Blair—had been frightened by it. She enjoyed fear in a way that fascinated and repelled him. It was at its prompting that she had made this the manner of their meeting; it was what lay perhaps at the bottom of their relationship. She had insisted that the sound was from a car on the coast road; that it was her husband; that it meant discovery, confusion. And she had clung to him. He had known very well that the sound came from off-shore, that it was the pulse of turbines in some steamer moving down the coast. And then it had stopped and she had been reassured. It had seemed to *stop*—he now remembered—rather than to fade into distance. This new sound, although also from the sea, was very different. It was the rapid throb of a motor-boat. And it was coming nearer.

The man from the sea took a great breath and stumbled forward once more. It was when only his ankles remained in water that Cranston hit on the truth about him. He was a fugitive.

He was a fugitive. That was why the engines had ceased. The man had swum from a steamer out at sea, and it had stopped and sent a launch in pursuit of him. The discovery drew from Cranston a confusion of responses. Here was something vexatious, frustrating—perhaps dangerous. His meeting with Caryl—their assignation, in the dark word that still excited him—was suddenly a mess. This encounter had ruined it, and presently they must manage to scramble out of its mere embarrassment and indecency as he himself must scramble into his shorts. For a moment he was aware only of what he was going to miss, and he felt his body tremble in what he took to be indignation or rage. But it wasn't that—or not wholly. Even as he stared at the other naked man he recognised within his own physical response a thrill of pleasure. What had risen from the sea was some harsh male predicament to which he responded as to a release.

The throb of the motor-boat was louder, as if the craft had rounded some point near at hand. And the man from the sea turned upon Cranston with an urgent and commanding gesture. The little sandy bay, pale as a bleached bone tossed against the dark cliff, was flanked at either end by a tumble of dark broken rock, and into gaining the shelter of the nearer of these refuges the man was now throwing his last energies. But he had also managed this imperious wave. Cranston was to go into hiding too. The motor-boat, if it appeared, must find only an empty beach.

This much was clear—and so was the proper immediate response to make. As Cranston ran for the rocks he felt again the flush of unreasonable pleasure. A problem had bobbed up from the blue—literally from that—and this time he knew the answer. Of course the man must be given a chance to explain himself. Even if some lurking risk were involved, he must be given a chance. To wait for the motor-boat, to haloo at it, would be treachery. It was surprising to Cranston that he should have this clear bit of knowledge, and surprising too that in the hurry and huddle of this strange flight it should rise up in his mind as a fact that was lucid and important. Moreover, it had so risen up without any visible basis in reason. The fellow now by chance at his side had no conceivable claim on him—and it was long odds, too, that he was simply some sort of commonplace wrong-doer. Treachery meant the breaking of a bond, and here no bond could possibly exist. Then why . . .?

They had made it. Their feet lost the firm sand and slipped on slime, trod painfully on barnacled rock. It was necessary to climb, but even some way up there was no more than bare cover for the two of them, and as they crouched down together in a shallow cup of darkness they had to press so close that each for a moment could hear the other's heart. Then the sound of the motor-boat drowned this and their rapid breathing. Cautiously Cranston moved his head a couple of inches to peer round a boulder. At the same moment the engine stopped. The boat had entered the bay on a long curve and was coming directly towards them now. As many as three or four men were crouched aft, and another man stood poised in the bows, sweeping the shore through night-glasses. For perhaps half a minute he scanned the farther rocks. Cranston remembered Caryl. She must have heard the engine, and presumably she was lying low there at the other end of the beach. He wondered what would happen if she lost her head and made a dash for his protection. He wondered what this boat-load of mysterious searchers would make of that surprising appearance.

The man with the glasses swung them round and appeared to focus straight on Cranston. Instinctively the young man drew back his head and shoulders, and the movement caused him to jostle his companion. Caught off balance, the man from the sea swayed and was about to tumble over the lip of the narrow depression in which they cowered. Cranston grabbed at him and caught first a naked shoulder and then an arm. For a moment the two men clung together, steadying themselves, and for the first time their eyes met directly. Here in the rocks they were in near-darkness, and what Cranston was aware of was no more than a fleeting intent gaze in a featureless face—a mere glint of light, no more, upon dilated pupils. But he knew that a signal, a sort of recognition, had passed. It declared a union which, if quite impermanent, was for the moment primitive and absolute. Neither had spoken a word, had so much as attempted to whisper. The whole adventure, so far, had happened in silence. But now there were voices. They came from the boat.

At least three of the pursuers were talking. Their words came clearly over the water but were completely unintelligible. They were speaking in a foreign language unrelated to any of which Cranston had a smattering. Yet it was clear to him that they were arguing, and with the same caution as before he took another glance round the boulder. The man in the bows was pointing towards the rocks and seemed to be urging a landing. It was about this that there was a dispute. And now, almost at once, the man in the bows prevailed. The boat had not yet entirely lost its momentum, and at a touch on the tiller it turned slowly and glided towards the beach. And Cranston found himself reacting swiftly. His mind took a leap to the backdrop of this obscure drama in the line of cliff overlooking the bay. There were a dozen places where it could be negotiated, and lately he had come to know

9

them well. One of them lay almost directly behind this hiding-place. If the man from the sea could be guided up that at once—and in the moonlight there was no great difficulty—his chances of finally escaping would be good. Cranston had put out a hand to tug gently at the fugitive's arm when he was arrested by a fresh sound.

"*Dick-ee!*"

It was Caryl calling from the farther rocks. And her voice held nothing of the fright that might have been expected of it. It held only what, heard ten minutes before, would have sent him racing across the sand with a swimming head. Now it did something queer to his stomach instead.

"*Dick-ee . . . where are you?*"

Cranston heard the man beside him catch his breath. Perhaps it was at the new hazard that this irruption brought into the affair. Perhaps it was an involuntary male response to what Caryl could put into that sort of call. And the young man felt himself deeply flush, so madly incongruous with that summons was the new drama into which he had been caught up. Then he tried to think. It seemed incredible that Caryl should not have heard the motor-boat and the voices. But nothing about her was quite incredible; nothing could be quite incredible about a woman so astoundingly——

His mind stopped, astonished at itself. The important thing was to get the hang of the new situation, and act. And once more he peered out. The men in the boat had all turned and were gazing at the farther rocks. They had certainly heard that unexpected call, and now there could be little doubt that they were glimpsing the caller. Impatient of delay, Caryl had emerged from hiding. Where they had supposed solitude and their quarry there was suddenly this untoward vision. That they were disconcerted was evident at a glance. And in a flash it came to Cranston that they were no more within the pale of the law than was the man they were hunting. There was a very good chance that they could be stampeded.

And Cranston shouted. *"John . . . Harry . . . David! Here's a boat, chaps! Come along down!"*

He made the rocks ring with it—and was aware that the man from the sea had caught the idea and was lustily shouting too. The success of the stratagem was startling. The engine of the motor-boat leapt into life, and the craft first turned in a whirl of foam and then tore out to sea. Within a minute it had vanished.

"Dick-ee!"

This time there was no doubt of Caryl's fright. The note of it touched off in him the strong positive response that had been so singularly lacking a few seconds before. His sense of himself as her lover seemed to slip over his head and slide down his body like a shirt: he was startled at the queer aberration which had presented him with her image as astoundingly stupid. But she did get easily confused and scared. It was rotten luck that having been so generous, so marvellous, she should be caught up in this bewildering assault from the sea. He felt protectiveness rise in him—an easy, obliterating emotion. He rose to his feet and called across the bay—called out in urgent, robust reassurance. "Darling . . . it's all right!"

"Dick-ee, come quickly!"

"All right, Caryl. I'm coming. But stay where you are. There's a man here . . . a stranger."

There was silence—stricken silence—and he turned to scramble down the rock. The poor darling. The poor old darling. He was about to call out again when, for the first time, the man from the sea spoke.

"Where are your clothes?"

Cranston stopped, startled. From the moment that he had heard the voices in the motor-boat he had been taking it for granted that the fugitive was a foreigner. And he had jumped to a conclusion, too, about his class. He must be a common sailor, a steward, somebody of that sort, involved' in unknown shady business turned suddenly desperate. It was on the basis of these assumptions that he had felt his unaccountable impulse of solidarity with the man. But now the man turned out to be an Englishman— and an Englishman who might have been at his own school. For Cranston the consequence of this discovery, strangely enough, was an immediate distrust, expressing itself in a quick backward step. Both men were now standing up, and the stranger was in full moonlight down to the waist. Cranston's recoil completed the movement he had begun to a lower level of the rocks, and he was now looking at the man from the sea as one might look at a picture skied in an old-fashioned gallery. The effect was, in the old exact sense, picturesque. The background was of jagged rock and the empty vault of the night, sparsely pricked out by a few pale stars. Against this the man was posed naked in a symbolism that might have been Leonardo's: the flesh—enigmatic and evanescent— framed in the immensities of geological and astronomical time. Moreover, in his own figure he sustained the comparison. He was a common man neither in the sense that Cranston had assumed nor in any other.

"Where are your clothes?" The man from the sea repeated his question impatiently, as if he seldom had to ask for information twice. He was in his early forties—and the fact that he was old enough to be Cranston's father increased the young man's new sense of distrust. He experienced a strong instant persuasion that this was the wrong sort of person to come tumbling out of the sea on an obscure wave of melodrama. But there was something more—a further and somehow yet more disconcerting perception to which he was helped by his own very respectable cleverness. He was in the presence not simply of another clever man, far more mature than himself. He was in the presence of a strong capacious intellect.

"My clothes?" Cranston heard the words jerk out of himself. "They're no distance away—what I've got. I've been bathing."

"So have I. And we couldn't have chosen a better night."

The joke—if it was meant as that—held for Cranston no reassurance. For the first time there came home to him what the pitch of the fugitive's desperation must have been. The channel was a long way out. Even from the cliff, steamers following it were hull-down on the horizon. The man had done a terrific swim. And he was next to naked. Clothes were his first necessity. And in the pool of shadow in which he still stood there was probably quite a number of small handy boulders lying about. Cranston realised a sobre chance that, when he turned away, the man from the sea would grab one of these and hit him on the head.

"If you want clothes, we'll have to do some talking." Cranston heard himself with surprise—both for the words, which he had not premeditated, and for the tone, which was calm. The discovery that he could command a decent poise before a man who was disclosing himself as formidable brought back to Cranston the start of pleasure which had been his first response on tumbling to the stranger's plight. "But you'll have to wait a bit." The better to assure himself that he really had some grip of the situation, Cranston for the second time looked straight into the stranger's eyes. This time, the features surrounding them were distinguishable, and for an instant he imagined that they stirred at something in his memory. "You'll have to wait." He repeated it briskly. "I'm going across to those other rocks. There are things you've rather upset."

"So I gather." The man from the sea was impassive. "But you should get them straight, I think, inside ten minutes. I'll expect you back then."

"I'll come back when I can." Cranston stiffened under what seemed a threat.

"Thank you. I realise I'm not your only pebble on the beach." The voice was ironic. "But don't forget me altogether and clear out. It would be disconcerting if I had to follow you like this . . . back to civilisation."

Cranston, without replying, began to climb down to the beach. He did so slowly, since he felt it prudent to keep an eye on the other man still. "Stay just where you are," he called back.

"Certainly—for a few minutes." The torso of the man from the sea slipped down into darkness until only his head and shoulders showed in the moonlight. He had found something to sit on. "But you needn't, my dear young man, think I'm going to slug you. I value you too highly for that. And doesn't the mere suspicion make you out a rather fickle fellow? We were like blood-brothers, you know, only five minutes ago."

Again Cranston said nothing. But he felt irritated— partly at having his years condescended to, and partly from acknowledging the truth of what the man from the sea had divined. He completed his scramble, and felt his feet on the sand.

"I wonder why?" The voice of the man from the sea came to him now from above only as a meditative murmur.

"I wonder . . . can *you* be getting away with something too?"

The last throb of the motor-boat had faded, and the sea lay dim and empty on either side of the broad bright causeway thrown across it by the moon. When half-way down the beach Cranston swerved and ran for the cliff. The shorts and gym shoes which were all he had set out in on this warm night lay at an easily identified spot; within seconds he had them on and was running to the farthest rocks. "Caryl?" His voice was carefully without anxiety. "Come out . . . it's quite all right."

She appeared instantly—jumping a small rock-pool in her urgency and tumbling into his arms. "Dicky, Dicky—what is it? I don't understand. It isn't Alex?"

"Of course not. Nothing like that." He took her in a quick embrace. Her body, slim beneath the slacks and thick sweater into which it was huddled, trembled not with the excitement familiar to him but in simple terror. He felt for her a sudden enormous pity and compassion, holding no proportion either with the degree or occasion of her distress. He held, caressed, soothed her—murmuring all his private endearments, secret names. It was something he had been constrained to do before, and he had skill at it. Out of the force of his solicitude he strained that skill now, exploited it with all the resource of his quick brain. And suddenly the very effort of this produced, without a single premonitory flicker in consciousness, a complete revolution.

He *was* so skilful only because it was all—the whole damned thing—happening through his brain. In this infernal theatrical moonlight he was like an actor who has been sunk for a space in his part, but to whom detached consciousness has returned, so that he must simply get through his scene with what deftness rests in him. The very largeness of his emotion of seconds before had spoken of its instability; and all that he now felt was a sharp impatience. That—and the shocked sense of everything being in process of becoming different, as if experience had incontinently, treacherously turned upon him its other face. But for the moment at least he could shut out its new enigmatical lineaments and look only at the practical problem confronting him. "It's all right," he whispered, "—quite all right. Only something's happened that rather ditches us for to-night. A man from the sea."

"A man from the sea?" She was bewildered.

"Escaped from a ship—and swum ashore. That motor-boat was after him. It's gone. But the man's on my hands still. He's over there in the other rocks."

"What sort of a man? What's it about?"

He shook his head. "I don't know. Smuggling, perhaps. I believe various up-to-date varieties exist."

"But how stupid!" Her confidence was returning. "He must go away. You must send him away."

"I don't know if I can." He hesitated. "And I want to know about him."

"But he has nothing to do with *us*!" It came from her as if proving that he had said something strictly nonsensical. "Please, please, Dicky, go and get rid of him. . . . I've only a little time. I must be going back." Her voice had gone husky, and she moved in his arms—with calculation, some new perception told him, so that through the thick wool her skin slid beneath his fingers. "Or can't we just slip away—into the field above the cliff?"

"I've got to find out about him." He saw that she was surprised as well as puzzled, and it came to him humiliatingly that here was the first indication she had ever

16

received that he had a will of his own. He was prompted to add: "And get him clothes."

"But he may be a criminal!" Caryl was horrified. "And you would be breaking the law. Dicky—do, *do* let us clear out."

Cranston let go of her and stepped back. She was at least tolerably secure again on her own pins. "I don't know that we could if we would. He's keeping an eye on us, I suspect. And he's prepared to make trouble if we don't toe the line."

"Make trouble?"

She was scared again—so that instinctively he put out a hand to her once more. "He's an educated man, and nothing escapes him. He sees that we wouldn't care for a lot of shouting."

"Why should we be afraid of it?" Abruptly, as if to enhance his sense of some horrible disintegration, she was spuriously bold—dramatic on a note that was wholly false. "I'd take it—with you, Dicky. I'd take *anything* with you. But I have to think of Sally."

It was the first time that she had spoken the name in weeks. He said very quietly: "Look—*you* can clear out. That will be the best thing, and at least it will cramp his style. Slip through the rocks to the cliff-path by the groyne. Then double back along the top to your bike and go home. I'll stay and deal with the chap."

For a moment he could see her waver. When she spoke it was with a queer desperation. "No. Not unless you go too."

"But surely——" He stopped—having caught suddenly at a fantastic truth. In her incredible head Caryl had fudged up some crazy suspicion. Perhaps it was to the effect that he had been prompted to conceal a second mistress at the other end of the beach. More probably

what had peered out in her was without definable content
—a mere irresistible wash of undifferentiated sexual
jealousy. And at this, under a sort of cold inner light
flicked on by the absurd discovery, Cranston starkly
realised the simple truth over whose contours his mind had
been intermittently groping for days and nights. It was
as if his fingers had slid beneath a delusively seductive
garment and come on ice.

He was crazy himself. For weeks he had been indulging
in a bout of madness. A casual observer—and now there
was one—would see in it no more than a run-of-the-mill
indignity of late adolescence. But it wasn't that. It
wasn't remotely just what one might feel elated about or
ashamed of according to one's mood. It was entirely
different. He wondered if it was unwittingly that Caryl
had touched the unbearable quick of the matter only a
minute before. . . .

He caught himself up. Their situation demanded action
and not reverie. Something prompted him to turn his
glance back along the beach. "Well," he said, "it's too
late, anyway."

"Too late, Dicky?"

"He's grown tired of waiting. Here he is."

CHAPTER II

"But he's naked!"

She spoke in a quick prudish alarm which ought to have been funny. But again what Cranston felt was impatience. "He's not—for what it's worth. But he certainly can't get far dressed only in the ghost of a pair of pants." He paused, perplexed. "What can his plan have been, going overboard like that?"

"He hadn't one, I suppose. He was just escaping from some foreign ship. They do often pass quite close."

Cranston was silent. The man from the sea would never be without a plan. His mind was of a sort that made such a state of affairs impossible. Cranston was sure of this, even while realising that he could give no rational account of his certainty. He watched the man come straight across the beach, and it occurred to him that in this light he ought to look slightly unreal, uncanny. For the moon takes the weight and substance out of things, and relieves them of intent and relatedness. But the man was quite real and very purposive. He might have been a golfer—a professional golfer—marching after his ball in the cold concentration of an important match. And now he was up with them and speaking.

"I thought it better to come across. It can't be very long till dawn. And you are probably anxious to get home." He had looked first at Cranston, as if to an acquaintance by whom some ceremony of introduction should be performed. But when nothing came of this he turned with brisk ease—with what might have been an acknowledgement of the happy propriety of a less formal note—to Cranston's companion. "Although," he added, " it's a perfect night on which to be out."

For a moment Caryl Blair said nothing, puzzled by the flat conventionality of his tone—by its lack of the impertinence or urgency she had expected. But she was still afraid, and when she did speak fear made her forthright. "Who are you? Why are you here? Why were they hunting you?"

"These are very reasonable questions." He was looking at her steadily. "And the first brings me at once to something rather astonishing. We have, as a matter of fact, met before."

"Oh no! I'm sure we haven't." Caryl's voice came to Cranston as pitiably scared. "There's no possibility——"

"But indeed we have . . . Lady Blair."

She gave a gasp and shrank towards her lover. "Dicky," she whispered, "take me away . . . take me away!"

"But not in circumstances which would cause *you* to remember *me*." As if unaware of her reaction, the man from the sea continued on the note of polite talk. "A mere introduction—but I was far from likely to forget it." He looked at her directly again, and his voice carried the precise intonation that the urbane compliment required. "And I met your husband too on the same occasion. But not, I think"—and he turned to Cranston—"your son."

There was a blank silence, and then Cranston heard Caryl draw a long shuddering breath. It was oddly echoed by a tiny wave breaking on the beach. The man had hit upon a pretence at once deft and cruel—something before which she was helpless, like one suddenly offered an insulting charity. And Cranston, determined that this make-believe should get no further, broke in. "You may as well know——"

"At something of the Royal Society's, would it have

been?" The man from the sea ignored the interruption. "Certainly it was some rather grand affair, at which I was surprised to find myself. You were wearing diamonds. That interested me, I need hardly say."

"My diamonds interested you?" Caryl had sufficiently recovered her nerve to tumble into vacuous curiosity. "I don't see why they should."

The man from the sea smiled. It was not, Cranston thought, a real smile. Indeed, nothing that he said or did was quite real; only his presence—his enigmatical presence—was that. And now for a fraction of a second he seemed to hesitate, as if debating some disclosure that it might, or might not, be expedient to make. When he spoke again, there was for the first time the hint of some concession to the dramatic in his voice.

"You were wearing uncommonly fine diamonds. But nothing like so fine, Lady Blair, as I am wearing now."

Again it should have been a funny moment. Caryl Blair, although she had all the careful modesty of an unchaste woman, looked the almost naked man up and down, round-eyed. "*Wearing* diamonds?"

He tapped his waist, and Cranston was once more aware of the belt he had first noticed as the man rose from the sea. The belt was bulkier—and the man himself more youthfully slim about the tummy—than had become apparent before. "You mean you *carry* diamonds?" Cranston asked.

The man from the sea nodded. "It's my trade. I work at this end of some rather large-scale I.D.B."

Cranston could see Caryl's eyes grow yet rounder. It struck him—and simply as one further confounding revelation—that her facial expressions were all conventional muscular manœuvres, picked up from plays and films, imagined from books. But her interest was genuine, and it was clear that this mysterious talk of diamonds held for her the same sort of fascination that an actual outpouring of gems themselves would have, were the stranger to tumble them out before her, all ice and fire beneath this ghastly moon. "I.D.B.?" she asked.

"Illicit diamond buying." The man from the sea, it seemed to Cranston, might have been saying "I work at the F.O." or even "My job's with I.C.I.—no reason why you should have heard of it, but it has to do with chemicals and things of that sort." He was entirely bland. And now he spoke again. "I'm afraid that to-night you've come up with—well, somebody doing what's scarcely expected of him." He gave Cranston a swift sardonic glance. "You mightn't believe it—but it does happen from time to time."

There was another silence—but not because Caryl made anything of this. Chinese would have meant no less to her. She turned to Cranston. "Then it *is* just smuggling? Not anything criminal?"

"Perhaps it can be put that way. But, if we help our friend here, we are certainly liable to be put in gaol—and after a picturesque joint trial. Can't you see us side by side in the dock?" He stopped—astonished at himself and suddenly ashamed. He had never before spoken to her meaning to hurt, and it seemed to him incredibly mean. For he was clinging to the cloudy notion that she had made for him some enormous sacrifice, and that he ought to be her man to the death. Yet there she was, a woman of about the same age as the stranger beside her, dressed in a sweater and slacks, and with an empty head. He glimpsed the terrifying fact that one creates and uncreates as one goes along; that one cannot help it; that fatuities and disenchantments and treacheries are regular byproducts in the queer chemistry of living.

"I'm afraid that is perfectly true." The man from the sea struck smoothly in, like a skilled family friend sensing domestic friction and unobstrusively pouring oil. "Fortunately, detection is unlikely. Indeed, it's scarcely an exaggeration to say that it hardly ever happens—at least as long as one's brains continue to work." He was mildly humorous. "And I think ours will do that."

"Was your brain working when you jumped overboard in your skin? " Cranston turned on him swiftly. "Is it your regular technique? Do you reckon to crawl gasping from the sea and stumble straight upon people like—like ourselves, every time?"

"That would be to expect too much altogether." The stranger's humour was a shade broader. " You weren't in my mind at all."

"Then what was in your mind? You seem to me to have done something quite desperate."

"There was a decided emergency. A matter of three or four friends of mine being suddenly prompted to cut my throat. It happens—in I.D.B. I jumped."

"With any plan?"

"Dear me, yes. One can't set out to swim an unknown number of miles in a lounge suit or a dinner jacket. But, once ashore, I was sure I could find a bathing-beach in time And there I could lie about unregarded all day in next to nothing—and until somebody proved a little careless of their clothes. Everything would be simple after that. I have plenty of money."

"Then you had better carry on. We won't stop you." Cranston hesitated. "Or say anything, either."

"That's right." Caryl joined in eagerly. "Go at once. And we'll say nothing. On our honour."

"Ah—on that." The man from the sea looked at Cranston inscrutably. "I wonder whether you—or your mother—can think of a better way in which I might get hold of some clothes?"

"I'll get you clothes." Cranston spoke coldly. He knew the man from the sea to be under no misconception about his relationship with Caryl, and his continued affectation in the matter was part of what appeared his pervasive falsity. Even his diamonds were surely false—and whether false or real they belonged to some small world of low criminality. Cranston felt that the man from the sea had in an indefinable way let him down. Nevertheless—if yet more indefinably still—there remained between them something that Cranston felt as a bond. He would have liked to break it—and now he was trying to see it as some sort of measurable obligation. Let him hand over so much, and he would be quits. Let him get the man from the sea inside a suit and walking upon leather—and that would be the end of him. "I'll get you clothes," he repeated. "I'll take you home and fit you out at once."

"But Dicky—you can't!" Caryl had grabbed him by the arm—and now, absurdly dragging him a few paces away, she fiercely whispered. "Dicky, it's too risky . . . the village . . . your people . . . you mustn't."

"It can't be helped, I'm afraid."

"We must take him the other way—mine. It's far safer. I can go ahead and get some of Alex's things. He'll never miss them. I'll leave them in the summer-house—the one by the cliff. Follow with him—and when he's dressed get him away. And meet me, Dicky—meet me to-morrow night."

"Very well." He knew it at once to be the better plan; that on a sober calculation it involved her in less ultimate risk than did his own. And he turned to the man from the sea. "We've fixed it up. Within an hour you'll be clothed —and gone."

"I mean to go ahead—but only to get things ready." Caryl added her explanations. "And I'm quite good at men's clothes. You can trust me."

"I'm sure I can, Lady Blair."

"Then I'll go." She had winced again at his knowledge of her name, as if feeling that it vastly increased his power to harm. "And we won't breathe a word. Only there must be a bargain."

"A bargain, Lady Blair?"

"Never mind." Before his polite blankness she was confused. By to-morrow, Cranston thought, she might be believing that they really had been taken for mother and son out on some innocent nocturnal skylarking; that no bargain had been in question; that they had helped the fugitive out of the bounty of their own romantic feelings. . . . And now she was still lingering. She still had something to say—and such was his pained sense of a large new knowledge of her that he was surprised at having no notion of what it could be. She was looking almost shyly at the man from the sea. "Will you show them to me?" she asked.

For a second it left Cranston merely wondering. The stranger was not at a loss. "I wish I could. But they are rather particularly sewn up, you know." Once more he tapped his belt. "And you couldn't tell them from pebbles."

"Pebbles?" She was naïvely astonished.

"They look no more than that—until they're cut."

"I see." She was like a child whom some prosaic fact betrays in the legitimate expectation of pleasure. "Where do you take them to?"

"Hatton Garden. All diamonds go there."

"So they do." She accepted this sagely. "But they will come back to you later—I mean the same ones?"

"Yes, I shall have further dealings with them later on."

"They'll be for sale?" She hesitated. "I could perhaps buy one or two—just by way of remembering this funny night?"

"It could be managed. Perhaps we might meet and discuss it some time." The stranger's tone continued to be conventional—so that Cranston supposed him quite unsurprised. Cranston himself felt his head swimming. He had good reason to know that Caryl's mind could very queerly veer about. But this freak was unbelievable. Or was it? She was silly about gems, and there was a bit of an explanation in that. Perhaps—he found himself considering this quite dispassionately—she was inevitably silly about men who rose gleaming from the sea in the small hours or presented any similar bizarre interest. But of more certain relevance was the fascination she found in funk. The man from the sea was frightening, and there was a good nine-tenths of her which this whole encounter prompted to mere flight. But some tiny remaining component wanted to stay and dabble . . . like this. Here on the familiar beach she had enjoyed her fill of one sort of delicious apprehensiveness. And now—perhaps without awareness of what drove her—she was reaching out to the man from the sea for another.

And Cranston's impatience was suddenly acute. A pair of diamond cuff-links would make a nice Christmas present for Alex. He heard the low pleasantry enunciate itself inside his head; and although he had no impulse actually to speak the words he flushed at them. It was true that everything had turned abominable. For a moment he believed that his consciousness of this was affecting him physically—had set a pulse throbbing at his temple. Then he realised that he was hearing, once more, something far

26

away. The throb was from a steamer out in the ocean-channel. And it had begun quite suddenly. The engines that had stopped half an hour ago were in action again.

The sound cut Caryl short. Perhaps the image of the invisible ship, variously manned and purposively moving, brought the outer world in its threatening aspect more sharply home to her. She turned away from the man from the sea—and a last quick scrutiny of his stripped body was perhaps only to tell her which of Alex's clothes would fit. "Dicky," she whispered, "—till to-morrow!" Then she vanished among the rocks. A minute later there was a glimpse of her—all tight slacks and voluminous sweater—scrambling clear of them and making for the cliff. The two men were quite silent. Only when the slow sea gave its next soft sigh their eyes met. They might have been acknowledging something appropriate in the sound.

"We'll give her twenty minutes." Cranston spoke prosaically. "For time, I think, isn't a worry. The nearest railway-station is about five miles up the glen. And there will be nothing odd about your strolling up to it in time for the first train."

The man from the sea nodded. "Nothing at all—provided the clothes are a reasonable fit."

"Blair's things will fit you, all right."

"Blair? Your— —?"

"Drop that, please." Cranston was surprised to hear his own voice tremble with anger. "You understand what—what you've seen, very well."

"I don't altogether understand *you*." The man from the sea spoke soberly. "Are you, I wonder, just a very great young puritan? Or is there something more?"

"I don't know what you mean." Even as he uttered the words, Cranston realised that they were the first lie he had spoken that night. And on this it came to him, as a linked and answering discovery, that the man from the sea had lied a great deal. "Let's stick to what's on hand, please. We've already made one slip."

"A slip?" The man from the sea was curious rather than alarmed.

"Shaving things. You won't look right in Blair's classy clothes and a day's beard. Perhaps——" Cranston stopped. His glance had travelled to the face of the man from the sea. Even by moonlight, it was possible to distinguish it as perfectly smooth.

"That's all right." The man was laughing softly. "I shaved before I jumped."

"While your friends were trying to cut your throat?"

"Precisely."

Again they were silent. The throb of the engines was fading. From what sounded almost as far away, a gull called and called again. Intermittently the sea, as if tired of a vain whispering in the ear of night, heaved itself into a larger wave which splashed on the pale beach like the smack of a drowsily amorous hand. A light breeze, faintly chill, was now blowing in from the ocean; it could be felt flowing past them—now fading to a breath and now growing to a small wind that would bend Jamieson's corn and Neil Clark's barley, that would rustle in the grasses of the old glebe where Sir Alex Blair's men might be mowing in the morning. It was strange to Cranston that in the familiar terrain he should suddenly be jostled by so much that was alien and inscrutable. The man from the sea was that. He presented indeed a front that was comprehensible enough—that was as dull as greed and as small as cheating. But behind him—Cranston perfectly knew—was some large hinterland of darkness. And it had been Cranston's immediate intuition of this that had given him the first sick sense of another vista. The affair with Lady Blair—so bewilderingly exciting and yet so finite as to be measurable in terms of mere minutes and inches—had its incalculable hinterland too. To put it bleakly, he had made a shocking mistake.

Cranston shivered—and if it was partly at his own train of thought it was nevertheless substantially because of what the breeze was doing to his skin. The night—all this succession of Scottish nights—had been incredible. His limbs had moved in an unreal medium, more balmy than any actual air, as if he had slipped into some travel advertisement in a glossy American magazine. But in the small hours there came an honest northern chill, and it was licking at him now. He had emerged cold from his short wallow in the sea, and nothing had happened at all to warm him up since. At twenty-two, such sensations resolve themselves into simple and immediate impulse. Cranston knew that he wanted to run. He wanted, if possible, to race. Almost theatrically, his world was darkening round him—but nevertheless he wanted the blood to be moving faster in his veins. He looked at the man from the sea.

He remembered that the man *was* from the sea. He had been in it for a long time—had in fact been very near never coming out of it. He, far more than Cranston, should be shivering now. But if he even felt the chill he gave no sign of it, and his naked poise was that of an athlete, despite his middle years. "What about a run to warm up?" Cranston asked.

"That's quite an idea." His idiom was Cranston's own, and as he turned lightly on his toes and glanced down the beach he might have been an undergraduate lazily ready for physical expression. He pointed to the other end of the beach. "There and back?"

"Yes." Cranston restrained himself from adding: "And I'll give you fifteen yards."

The man slipped off his belt and dropped it carelessly on the sand. "No point," he said, "in carrying weight. Will you give the word?"

"On your marks, get set, go?"

"Right."

For a moment more they parleyed over the form of the thing. They were like two boys from different public schools, rather warily meeting in the holidays and making their arrangements with punctilio. Then they were off. Cranston could tell at once that the man had been a sprinter. His own best distance was the half-mile. He gave himself to the serious business of running as fast as he could—thinking about his breathing, trying to avoid spots where the sand looked too soft to thrust from with the ball of the foot. The man from the sea was actually heading him; they were level at the turn by the farther rocks; Cranston led all the way back, but at the finish would scarcely have cancelled the fifteen yards' handicap he had rashly thought to offer. For some moments they stood panting. For a further second they turned to each other, laughing—as if experiencing again, less tensely, the odd intimacy that had surprised them as they lurked in hiding. And then the man from the sea stooped quickly, picked up his belt and fastened it round his middle. He glanced down as he did so, making sure of the buckle. And something pricked at Cranston's memory.

Once already he had experienced the sensation of near-recognition. This time it prompted him to speak. "You know," he said, "I don't believe a word of your story."

The man from the sea made one further movement, settling the belt about his waist. And then he stood quite still—and for so long that Cranston had the sense of

having uttered unwittingly the words of a potent im-
mobilising spell. They had been words prompted, at least
in part, by the obstinate irrational feeling that the man
from the sea had something to share with him. They had
borne—or been intended to bear—the character of an
approach to confidence, an appeal for candour. But they
were also the product—Cranston was conscious—of some
piece of crucial knowledge hovering just beyond his power
of recollection. Perhaps it was the nature of this—he
suddenly found himself rather urgently feeling—that now
gave them, retrospectively, the sense of being highly
injudicious.

"What's wrong with my story?" When he did speak,
the man from the sea spoke gently. At the same time he
took a couple of steps away from Cranston, so that the
rocks received him partly into their shadow and he became,
once more, like a picture cast in bold chiaroscuro. "You
interest me," he said mildly. "Just where does my story
strain credulity?"

"It's not your story; it's yourself." The race had not
only sent Cranston's blood coursing more swiftly. It had
quickened his brain. He had lately experienced novel
pleasures—but now an old one had with unexpected
suddenness returned to him. It was the clever schoolboy's
pleasure in his own powers—when only lately discovered
and still felt as a wonderful springboard to the world. He
remembered that his wits worked well—and at the same
time realised that for days, for weeks, they had hardly
been working at all. But they were coming back to him
now, and with them the power of lucid speech. "Or
rather," he said, "it's the lack of adequate correspondence
between the one and the other—between your story, you
know, and *you*. You're the wrong man for it—quite the
wrong man for that diamond-smuggling yarn. If I'd

31

thought to pick up that belt and hand it to you—and why in the world *didn't* I think of it?—there would have been nothing like the feel of gems beneath that webbing. It isn't even heavy; it didn't fall as if it were. Papers, perhaps, or banknotes well waterproofed. But *not* diamonds destined for Hatton Garden." He paused. "That's one thing."

"There are others?"

"I don't think you jumped into the sea because some chaps were then and there going to cut your throat. You jumped on a predetermined plan—and it included the efficient little detail of shaving immediately beforehand." Cranston paused. He was the schoolboy in the middle of a model construe. "You seem so efficient that I'm surprised you didn't get overboard more quietly, or in circumstances that would allow you more grace. Being chased up so quickly was, if you ask me, a poor show."

"It was a very uncomfortable one. Anything else?"

"No. But the point, I think, lies there. This diamond-smuggler in a professional way that you conjure up—he might well choose that desperate swim if there was really a knife at his throat. But he wouldn't plan it, have that tidy shave, and then jump in cold blood. It's a different order of person who'd do that. It's other motives that drive men to tricks of that sort."

"Is that so?" The man from the sea paused. It was something that he, too, knew how to do. "Would it be terribly impertinent to ask your age? This blending of the severities of logic with a ripe human wisdom makes me decidedly curious."

Cranston flushed. "I'm twenty-two," he said shortly.

"Twenty-two? So wise so young, they say, do never live long."

"I beg your pardon?" Cranston was startled.

"Something that an extremely sinister person was prompted to say about a very bright small boy. The story ended in the Tower of London. I hope neither yours nor mine will do that."

"There you are." Cranston made a bold bid for recovery. "Diamond-smugglers don't gabble Shakespeare."

The man from the sea nodded. It was his first movement for what seemed a long time. "It's not a bad point. . . . Are you just down from Oxford?"

"Cambridge."

"Then let me say that your intelligence does your college credit. Your morals appear to be another matter." The man from the sea produced his softest laugh. "And how, my dear boy, you feel it!"

"My affairs aren't really the question, are they?"

"Do you know—I believe *that* a little remains to be seen?" The man from the sea stepped forward again— and contrived to make the action suggest some marked drop in tension. "By the way," he said, "isn't it about time we were going after those clothes?"

"More than time." Cranston took a last glance at the empty beach and then turned towards the rocks. "It's a bit of a scramble in places. I'll go ahead."

For some seconds they moved in single file through deepening shadows. When the man from the sea spoke again it was on a practical note. "Do they have dogs?"

"The Blairs? They have several. But I don't think they'll make a row."

"I suppose they're used to a certain amount of nocturnal traffic."

Cranston said nothing. He hated the joke—and hated himself for having no right to resent it. And he felt that it was not made for its own sake. The man from the sea

33

didn't really have any humour in him. But he had plenty of subtlety. If he irritated you, it was by design.

"Is it a large household?"

"No—quite small." Cranston answered without turning his head.

"There isn't what I so tactfully tried to take you for—a grown-up son?"

"No." Cranston felt his anger mounting.

"Ah—childless. That's where to look for a maternal mistress."

Cranston stopped and swung round. "She's not childless, blast you. There's . . . a grown-up daughter. Hers—not his."

They had emerged from the rocks, and the moonlight fell full upon the face of the man from the sea. He said nothing, and his features remained entirely impassive. But after a moment he gave a slight nod—as a person might do who has solved some very simple problem along expected lines. The two men looked at each other—it was another of their odd exchanges—and then turned and walked side by side towards the cliff.

CHAPTER III

THE ATTACK came seconds later and took them both utterly by surprise. Cranston was not to know the man from the sea so caught unawares again. Even so, he acted very quickly—taking Cranston to momentary safety in a rugger tackle as he went down himself. It was in the hollow of dry loose sand immediately below the cliff; they lay prone in it as the second batch of bullets kicked and spat about them or whined over their heads. In the sudden unbelievable crisis Cranston found his mind working fast. Apparently fear was like a wound, and took time to make itself felt. It had got no grip yet. But in a matter of minutes—if he *had* minutes—it would be humiliatingly at work on him. Meanwhile the initiative was his. He knew the ground. "Are you all right?" he asked.

"Yes—but can we get clear?" The voice of the man from the sea was calm. "They must have landed somebody before making off back to the ship. Silly to think there's magic in British soil. But my guess is that it's only one chap."

"It's one chap, all right—and with some sort of tommy-gun out by the point. If we can make the cliff we've a chance. The path cuts through it so that there's nearly always at least a foot or two of cover from down here."

"Good. We'd better make the dash now. If we stop, the blighter has only to walk up to us and blow our brains out. On your mark?"

Cranston heard himself laugh—and distrusted the sound. "Get set," he said. His finger-nails were digging into his palms, and it was with an effort that he flattened

35

his hands on the sand to get better purchase for a spring. He drew up one knee beneath his belly and tensed his whole body. From behind him he fancied he heard the scrape of booted feet on rock.

"Go!"

They were up and running—and instantly the bullets were spitting and singing again. The man from the sea went down and rolled in sand. There was another burst and he gave a sharp cry of pain. The fear Cranston had been expecting pounced. It came as a sickening physical clutch at his bowels and reins. But he found that he had stopped and was trying to heave the man from the sea into cover that was now only a few yards away. There was another spray of bullets which for some reason flew wide. The man from the sea was on his feet again and running. There was something odd about him, but he was making it. They had both made it. On one side of them was the main face of the cliff and on the other an almost continuous breastwork of rock, to keep in the shelter of which they had barely to stoop. Cranston thrust the man from the sea before him. "Up you go," he said. "You can't miss it."

They climbed—but to Cranston's mind too slowly. "Speed up," he whispered. "But quietly. It's only if he wastes time finding the path that we've a chance."

"Get ahead of me, will you?" The voice of the man from the sea was still calm. "It was a graze on the ankle that brought me down. But the real mischief's my eyes."

"Your eyes?" As he scrambled ahead Cranston felt a queer chill.

"One of those bullets spat sand into them far too hard to be comfortable. I can't see a thing. But I can follow you well enough."

Suddenly Cranston felt himself rebel—rebel against the

36

grotesque destiny that a brief hour had brought upon him. If he stuck by the man from the sea he was almost certainly going to be killed—and without so much as knowing why. It was true that in some brief span of months or years any one of a variety of horrible deaths might come to him. His whole generation walked day by day in the consciousness of that. But death in battle would be death with others of his own sort—and in a cause at least approximately definable, so that there would be a sort of meaning in it. In this there was no sense at all. It was going to be like a street accident. And he was going to be dead. Dead at twenty-two. Because of having got mixed up with some sort of crook. . . . Cranston looked at the cliff-face on his left. He could turn aside and scale it. The light was quite good enough. He would be out of this nightmare just as quickly as he had been in. And the man from the sea could settle his own account.

Suddenly he was shivering from head to foot. It was as if these thoughts were equivalent to finding himself out on the verge of the cliff in a great wind, with his balance swaying. For a second the image held him paralysed. And then, oddly, it prompted him to think ahead and to speak. "Listen—there's only one dangerous place. It's about fifty yards in front of us and half-way up. The path takes a turn on an overhang, and for perhaps a dozen feet it curves round with no protection on the outer side at all. But I'll face round and keep a hand on your right shoulder —and you'll keep your left dug into the cliff. All right?"

"All right."

They continued to scramble. Again Cranston thought he heard the scrape of boots, and from almost directly below. His heart sank. If they could gain a sufficient start there was a chance that they might successfully go to earth somewhere on top. But if the fellow found the path and sighted them before they were clear of the cliff, then they were certainly done for. At the top he would have them in a narrow cleft and with the moon dead ahead. A single burst from that gun would settle the matter.

And now they had come to the ugly bit. The natural parapet on their right had vanished; for four or five yards the path ceased to be through the cliff and wound on a steep curve sheer across its face. Cranston turned round and dropped on all fours. The man from the sea was already crawling. Working backwards was not difficult in itself, but it was less easy when he had to keep one guiding hand almost constantly on the other's shoulder. And suddenly their pursuer made himself unmistakably heard. He was on the path and coming up rapidly. Their plight was hopeless.

Cranston looked to his left and down. They were out on the over-hang, and the moon-blanched sea lay directly below. He wondered what would happen if one took a dive from a height like this. Probably one's body would lose all control of itself and hit the surface in a fashion that would immediately kill. Anyway, there were rocks. He could see them just beneath the surface, like green veins in a milky marble. . . . They went on crawling. He avoided looking directly into the face of the man from the sea, because even in this horrible situation there was a further horror in the thought that the man was perhaps blinded. Once, the man's right knee slithered under him on some treacherously worn patch of the path, and Cranston thought that they were both going over. Then a shadow loomed behind his own left shoulder. It was the parapet again. Their death wasn't to be by water.

But now their pursuer was upon them. He was somewhere just short of the hazard they had so painfully negotiated. And they were utterly helpless. He was again

1 the position that the man from the sea had crisply de-
.ined. He had nothing to do but walk up and blow their
brains out.

The path was less steep and they had got to their feet.
There were at least a few more paces that they could take,
and it seemed a point of honour to take them. Cranston
had the man from the sea by the hand. And suddenly he
realised that they were in almost complete darkness.

It was the point at which the path turned again sharply
into the cliff—and its direction was such that, for no more
than a matter of feet, the clear moonlight made no impression on its shadows. But in another couple of yards
there would be no shadows at all. Cranston stopped,
turned, and took a couple of backward paces. As he edged
past the man from the sea his mouth was close to his ear.
"It's the only place," he whispered.

"To fight?"

"To have a shot at it."

"He's more likely to have several shots at us."

"Ssh!"

From quite close to them there had come the rattle of a
pebble displaced on the path. Cranston took one further
backward step and had before him a panel of moonlight
and a strip of sea. It was the last few feet of that hazardous
curve. If the man with the gun could be stopped anywhere, it was decidedly here. Cranston turned to claw
at the cliff face for a loose stone, a clot of clay. And as he
did so the man appeared.

The moonlight fell upon him as for a photograph. He
had rounded the curve and was standing still, so that for a
moment he was like a dummy in a tailor's window. And
the first thing noticeable was his clothes. They were
absurdly urban to have come direct from ship-board.
Moreover, the man himself had the same suggestion. He

39

was plump and pale—and he was peering into the shadows through rimless spectacles and from beneath a trilby hat. The whole appearance thus presented was so incongruously mild that Cranston for a moment felt almost persuaded that there must be some bizarre mistake. Then he saw that the man really had a gun. He was raising it now. He knew just where his quarry lurked. He was making his kill.

Something came free under Cranston's fingers. It was about the size of a cricket-ball. He looked fixedly at the man's spectacles glinting with a sort of treacherous reassurance in the moonlight and tried to imagine them a pair of bails. The distance wasn't much farther than from cover-point. He raised his arm. The movement must have betrayed him, for in the same instant the man levelled his gun—a glinting short-barrelled affair. There was no time for a moré careful aim, and Cranston threw. The stone—for it was that—had scarcely left his hand when he knew that it was going wide. And he would never have a chance to reach for another. The stone was flying wide of the spectacles by eighteen inches—by a couple of feet. And then he saw the gun magically flicked from the man's hands, and in the same instant heard a sharp crack. The stone had taken it on the muzzle and it was spinning in air. A fraction of a second later there was a tiny splash. The weapon was in the sea. The enemy had been disarmed.

"Can we go for him?" It was the man from the sea who spoke. Whether or not his sight was coming back to him, he appeared to know perfectly what had happened. "Could we chuck him into the water?"

"I could take him over with me—like Sherlock Holmes with Dr. Moriarty." Cranston was moved to sudden sarcasm. "And then you could just carry on. Shall we try that?"

"Or have you a knife?" The voice of the man from the

...ea was quite level. "Could we collar him lower down and cut his throat?"

"He looks as if he'll just clear out. Won't that do?"

"I'd rather we killed him."

Cranston was silent. He realised that the man from the sea meant precisely what he said. And this realisation, more than the deadly danger he had himself been in seconds before, brought home to him the queer fact that he had dropped into an utterly unknown world. It occurred to him that the man with spectacles might have another weapon—perhaps a revolver—and that it was of this danger that the man from the sea was thinking. But there was no sign of anything of the sort. For a further couple of seconds their late pursuer held his ground—harmlessly and irresolutely, like a pedestrian become aware of being in the wrong street or meditating a cautious encounter with a stream of traffic. The circumstances of the affair seemed to require from him a grimace of rage, a howl of baffled fury. But all that the man with the spectacles did was to clear his throat as if about to address the darkness. No words came—and the commonplace sound was followed by a gesture yet more uncannily commonplace. The man produced a handkerchief, removed his trilby hat and mopped his forehead. Then he replaced the hat, stowed away the handkerchief, turned, and walked off down the path. In a second he had vanished; for some seconds more they could hear his composed retreat; and then that was the end of him. Cranston was alone with his first and equally problematical companion.

"I can see the moon—or at least I'm aware of it." The man from the sea was moving forward cautiously, his hand on Cranston's arm. "But that's all. It presents a complication."

"In getting to Hatton Garden?"

"We've agreed, I think, that Hatton Garden is a fiction." The man from the sea produced his accurately contrived yet spurious effect of humour. "I can't expect you to believe that diamond smugglers go to quite the lengths we've just been witnessing." He paused. "I wish that fellow hadn't got away."

"He can do more damage—arm himself again?"

The man from the sea shook his head. "He can contact . . . others. Again, it's a complication."

"There's the house." Cranston pointed, momentarily forgetful of his companion's condition. "We skirt this wall, and then go through a gate to the summer-house. The clothes will be waiting. And that will be a start. It could be an end, as far as I'm concerned, except for this business of your eyes. If you want more help, you must tell the truth."

"My dear young man!" The voice beside Cranston had taken on a tone of mock alarm. "That might be stiff, you know—very stiff, indeed. Patricide, fratricide and all unmentionable crimes may be on my hands."

"I'm bearing that in mind." Cranston spoke grimly.

"My advice to you is to give me more help—just a little more help—while asking no questions. It will be more comfortable . . . all round."

"Is that a threat again?"

"I suppose it is." The man from the sea paused. "Would you have Sir Alex Blair know?"

"Blast Blair."

"Or . . . the daughter?"

There was a long silence. Cranston was waiting for the blood to stop hammering in his head. "Aren't you," he asked carefully, "a pretty great blackguard?"

"I am what you knew me to be in the first minutes of our meeting. The right word for it is desperate. Do you know what it is to be desperate?"

"I'm learning."

The man from the sea had paused in his halting walk. Now he moved on. "One can talk to you," he said unexpectedly. "You're beyond your years."

"So wise, so young——?"

"You'll live long enough, so far as I'm concerned. It's not all that catching."

Cranston looked sharply at the man treading carefully beside him. But he could distinguish no play of expression accompanying this odd speech. What the moonlight did sufficiently reveal was the fact that the man's face was a mess. He must be in considerable pain—but after that first sharp cry he had given no sign of it. If he was a blackguard he was other things as well. And his real life—it came to Cranston—lay far below any facet of himself that he had yet revealed. He had come naked out of the sea—but in an impenetrable disguise. There was nothing about him that one could be sure of—except some underlying intensity of purpose, some dark obsession, which it was impossible to define. There was that—and there was this last queer little speech. It had seemed to slip up, eluding the vigilance of some censor, from a hitherto hidden stratum of his mind. But even of that one could not be certain. The man from the sea was subtle and formidable. His most spontaneous-seeming utterance might be a premeditated and planted thing.

"We go through here." Cautiously, Cranston eased open a door in the high stone wall. "I hope I'm right about those dogs. Better take my hand again. There's a winding path to the summer-house. I can just make it out. The moon's going down."

"And that means dawn in no time. We can be clear in half-an-hour?"

"We could be. But it all needs thinking about. And what's possible depends upon the truth of your situation, you know, and the risks you may actually have in front of you." Cranston was briskly practical. "That's why it's just no good keeping me in the dark."

"I wish I could keep myself there. Is this summer-house we're making for safe?"

"No one comes near it, day or night. It's perfect for——" Cranston broke off, and he knew that his cheeks had flushed as at a monstrous recollection. "The house is a quarter of a mile away. It's got enormous grounds."

"Of course Blair is wealthy as well as scientifically distinguished." The man from the sea had turned on his note of irony. "I remember how your friend's diamonds proclaimed the fact at that reception."

"Did you say the Royal Society?" Cranston scarcely knew why he asked the question. But even as he uttered it he acknowledged that it was significant—that his mind by means of it was taking a dive at some submerged memory.

The man from the sea made no answer—perhaps because he had almost stumbled at a turn of the path. When he recovered himself it was to speak in a tone of impatience. "Aren't we nearly there?"

Cranston in his turn was silent. The garden was warm and scented and very still. The breeze from the sea had either dropped or was here deflected by the sweep of the cliff. The scents were the unique mingling he had known from childhood in such rare northern gardens as this: lavender and roses and sweet briar and night-scented stock shot with the sharpness of the sea and the tang of the surrounding pine and heather. It was a heady mixture.

44

Eden, it queerly occurred to him, had been eminently aromatic—and but for that Eve might never have eaten her apple there. His own apple—— Cranston caught himself up. With an appropriateness that was sufficiently broad, the familiar summer-house had loomed up before him. "We're there," he said briefly. "I don't know about risking a light. We'll see when we get in."

They mounted the little flight of steps and passed across the broad verandah. The summer-house was an elaborate and expensive affair, commodious but without appropriateness to its situation. There was a large dark central room that might have been intended as a refuge from tropical heat, and from the shadowy corners of which it was possible to picture the emergence of exotic persons in the tradition of Conrad or Somerset Maugham. And there was such a presence now—a vaguely defined form in white, that stirred and rose as they entered, and then stood still.

Cranston was startled. "Caryl! You've waited? We've been——"

The figure in white took a single step forward, and spoke very quietly. "I'm not Caryl. I'm Sally."

CHAPTER IV

"Mother sprained an ankle coming up the path. She could hardly get as far as the house." Sally Dalrymple continued to speak from the darkness. Her voice was slightly tremulous and slightly hurried, as if she were determined not to be interrupted before she had declared herself. "So she tumbled me out of bed. She'd had one of her bouts of sleeplessness, she said, and had gone to walk on the beach. And she'd run into you, Dick, with a friend in some sort of fix. It wasn't very clear—but I was to bring these clothes. Is that right?"

There was a silence—a silence that Cranston knew it was his business to break. But his mouth had gone dry, and he felt as he had sometimes felt when half awakening from a ghastly dream. In the dream he had done he hardly remembered what. But it could never be undone. *Never.* And its aftermath was dread and dereliction and dismay.

"The clothes are right, at least." It was the man from the sea who spoke—striking in with the hateful urbanity he could command. "From my point of view, they are the important thing. I have to be dressed in them."

"Then I hope they fit." Sally's voice was cold, and Cranston knew that she had instantly disliked the stranger. She distrusted him—and for the same reason that Cranston himself had felt a sudden distrust earlier. He was the wrong age to be in a fix with innocence, with any attractiveness as of mere escapade or extravagance. She had been trying to accept the situation as her incredible mother had launched it at her—and that meant a Dick Cranston involved in some hazardous silliness with a contemporary. Poaching, perhaps—or swimming out to Inchfail to play some prank on old Shamus in the lighthouse. But this smooth middle-aged man was inexplicable.

"I'm sorry about Lady Blair's ankle." Cranston spoke these words simply as being no worse than any others. Anything he said to Sally must be abominable. He realised—and his realisation was like a further turn of the screw—that he had no notion what Sally felt or believed. It seemed incredible that she shouldn't know the truth. But perhaps a girl like Sally was like that—incapable of conceiving evil, or that sort of evil. At least she must be on the brink of knowledge. And Caryl had put her there deliberately; had put her there with the particularly ugly deliberation of the unconscious mind. No doubt Caryl *had* sprained an ankle. But it was, at this moment, the ingenious thing to do. It had enabled her to play what he now understood to be her morbidly compulsive fear-game; to wake Sally with a story as thin as paper. Perhaps—for he felt his new view of Caryl becoming fuller and fuller— perhaps there was a sort of cruelty in it. Perhaps she enjoyed the thought of constraining her daughter desperately to repel what could be to her only a vile suspicion.

"Can I do anything more for your friend?" The girl asked the question carefully as if she were an agent only, involved in this nocturnal hugger-mugger simply because of an order that had come to her.

"He isn't a friend." Cranston swiftly spoke the truth where it could be spoken. "He's a stranger straight out of the sea, and he has a cock-and-bull story about smuggling diamonds."

"But I'm not sticking to it." The man from the sea spoke with an air of easy candour. "I don't smuggle diamonds."

"Then is it some sort of joke?" Sally turned towards Cranston in the darkness. "Or is he mad?"

"If he's mad then others are mad too. You didn't hear a racket?"

"Not that firing?" Sally spoke swiftly, so that he remembered with ignoble fear how intelligent she was. "It didn't sound like the usual stuff out at sea."

"It wasn't. It was a chap with a gun. And he tried it out on us."

For a moment she was silent. "Honour bright?"

It was an old challenge between them, and now he hated it. "Honour bright," he answered. "He ended by losing his gun. But he did some damage first."

"To you?"

His heart leapt in a sort of dreadful joy at something in her voice. "Not me."

"He got my eyes." The man from the sea had been very still in the darkness, and Cranston knew that he was making it his business to gather all he could of the relationship at play before him. But his speech was almost casual. "Only, I think, to the extent of bunging them up with sand. I hope I can get rid of it. For I have to get south, you see—and it will have to be done unobtrusively. Is there any water here?"

"I'll fetch water—and an eye-bath and lotion if I can find them." Sally became brisk and moved at once towards the door. She had her sex's instinct for practical action in any obscure exigency. "But I shall be at least a quarter of an hour. You can work out your plans together." She had given an edge to this—but now as she passed Cranston she whispered to him on another note. "Dick—are you really involved with him?"

"In a limited way, yes." This time he felt merely awkward. "But I know absolutely nothing about him."

48

"Then I don't see——" She checked herself. "And it's something that has to be kept from . . . Alex?"

She had made the little pause before her step-father's name by which she commonly seemed to distance him. He knew that for some reason she didn't find Alex Blair easy to take. "Yes," he said. "I think it better had be."

"Very well." She was suddenly indifferent. "There are cigarettes and matches on the table, if you want them. Although I can't think who put them there."

He was silent. Caryl and he had smoked three or four. It was a small squalid moment as in some low stage-play of adultery.

She turned away. And then suddenly she had turned back again and put out a hand. It touched his arm, his chest, and then without haste withdrew. She was laughing —innocently and genuinely amused. "Dick—have *you* no clothes on either?"

"Precious few."

"I'll bring something—a pullover."

"Alex's?"

"No!" He was startled, bewildered by the sudden passion in her voice. But she laughed again. "Something of my own. It won't be too bad a fit."

She was gone. For a moment he saw her as a mere white blur in the last faint moonlight filtering into the garden. But he saw her too in a sharp interior image, dressed for the moors—wholesomely broad at shoulders as well as hips. It was true that she could bring something that would fit well enough.

From behind him in the summer-house the man from the sea spoke composedly. "So far, so good. For me—and, I hope, for you."

"I'd have thought your chances were pretty thin."

49

Cranston spoke more from irritation than from any sense of a secure grasp of the affair. "You must be some sort of outlaw, I suppose, or you would already be taking steps to contact the police. And a helpless outlaw, too, as long as your eyes are out of action. What you have found, for the moment, is a very insecure refuge, indeed."

"One must look on the bright side." The man from the sea was quite invisible, but he appeared to have found somewhere to sit down in the darkness. "Not that realistic appraisal is not always valuable. Were you ever under fire before?"

"No—except for field-days. And with blanks."

The man from the sea laughed. "Then you did uncommonly well. But so, for that matter, did I."

"Have *you* never been under fire?"

"Decidedly not. You mustn't form, you know, too romantic a picture of me."

"I don't find you in the least romantic." Cranston spoke with conviction. "My guess is that you're some sort of paid spy."

"It sounds ugly. And yet I suppose all spies get pay. Is it your idea that the chap with the gun was from— what is it called?—M.I.5?"

"I don't know. And I don't know why he went off in that commonplace fashion."

"Because he wasn't—for him—doing anything very out of the way. He' could take no further effective action against us. So he simply passed on to the next thing."

"Which would be reporting failure? Would he go back to that ship?"

For a moment the man from the sea made no reply. When he spoke again his voice was slightly muffled, and Cranston caught a gleam from his naked shoulders unexpectedly near the floor. He must be sitting on some low bench or stool, with his head buried in his arms, and probably his eyes were hurting him badly. "The ship? I don't think so. It wouldn't linger. He was simply shoved ashore from the motor-boat before it went back to the ship, and told to do what he could. The people he will have to contact are now in this country."

"Doesn't that give you time?" Cranston felt for something on which to sit down himself. "I find it hard to believe that he can whistle up a whole like-minded gang out of the Highlands."

"It's an encouraging point." For the first time, the man from the sea let something like weariness tinge his irony. "But how boring this is. All about me. Let's talk about you—and the girl."

"Let's do nothing of the sort—and damn your impertinence."

Cranston took some satisfaction in coming roundly out with this. But the response of the man from the sea disconcerted him. "I'm sorry. I oughtn't to have approached it—or not in that way. But you've been rather a good show, you know, so far as I'm concerned. You've given me the deuce of a leg up—and for no earthly reason that I can see. So I didn't mean impertinence—only sympathy."

"I don't want sympathy."

"No more you do. I talk like an idiot. All long-distance swimmers are probably idiots." The man from the sea produced his phonetically perfect laugh. "But I think you might want—well, an objective appraisal. Are you in a mess? "

"You can see that I'm in a mess."

"Talked to anyone?"

"No."

"You love the girl?"

There was a silence. "Yes." Incredulously, Cranston heard his own voice ring out the word. "Yes. I do."

"She turned you down?"

"She turned me down. She had a right to, hadn't she?" He spoke savagely. "As a matter of fact, she was horrified."

"My dear lad!" The man from the sea appeared to be soberly unbelieving. "You can't mean horrified. It doesn't make sense."

"It had to make sense—to me. There it was. I'd thought—I'd thought it might be all right. And there it was—a ghastly flop. It must have been the last way she was prepared to think of me. And yet it wasn't . . . or I thought not." Cranston stopped, aware of his own incoherence. "That gun shook me, I suppose. I'm crazy to tell you this."

"Did you ever think to make love to a girl before?"

"No—I didn't."

In the darkness the man from the sea laughed softly, so that Cranston felt his cheeks suddenly burn. "My dear boy, I won't say of the virgin approach that it's a terrible mistake. But it invites disasters—and it's a matter of luck whether they turn out comic or tragic. You were utterly at sea. You hadn't a clue. And you missed out whole volumes in folio."

"I don't believe a healthy girl wants volumes in folio. But I expect I was"—Cranston hesitated—"clumsy enough."

"That was the whole thing." The man from the sea spoke with unemphatic conviction. "Think about her here—about her tone to you—a few minutes ago."

"I can't—I won't." It came from Cranston like a cry. "There can't have been a mistake—a misunderstanding. There mustn't. It would make it worse, far worse, unbearable."

"About the mother?"

"Yes." It took Cranston seconds to utter the word, and he did so tonelessly. "I turned cynical, vicious, crazy—and I went for her."

"What utter nonsense."

It was the man from the sea at his quietest, and it pulled Cranston up. "What do you mean? Do you think we haven't——? Do you think I'm boasting, telling some filthy lie?"

"I think you're flattering yourself." The man from the sea was amused. "About that access, I mean, of vicious, cynical activity. You were thrown off balance and the mother seduced you. It came to no more than that. You're about the age she goes for, I'd say. And if she virtually raped you from her own daughter—well, that was additional fun." He paused. "You know all this. You possess an active intelligence which has certainly got you straight about it by this time."

"Do you think you're being comforting?"

"I certainly hope so." The man from the sea sounded genuinely surprised. "It's the first stage with a problem isn't it?—to get the terms of it clear. And yours is not a very complex problem, you know. Ten minutes has served to see it as it is. Now you work out the solution. I wish my own conundrum were as simple."

"You talk as if it was all science."

"Of course it's all science. Anything in which the mind can establish causality is science—and nothing but science. And the solution of your problem is simple—as simple as a right-about turn."

"I just have to try again—and on some convenient future occasion tell Sally that once upon a time I was an ass?"

"In essence—yes." The man from the sea was still confident. "Of course, I'm not discounting emotional complications in what is itself an emotional matter. You must work out how to deal with them. Particularly the magical side."

"I don't know what you mean."

"The really primitive response in your situation, I imagine, is a kind of tabu response. You are inclined to imagine an absolute inhibition. The idea of first the mother——"

"For God's sake shut up!" Cranston found that he had been crouched on a wicker chair, and that now he had sprung up and was pacing the summer-house. A faint grey light was seeping into it, and he could distinguish the few pieces of neglected furniture scattered about. "Didn't Sally say there were cigarettes?" He fumbled at a table. "You can say that a feeling like that is magical, primitive, pagan, uncivilised. It's probably unchristian too, for all I know."

"It's certainly that." The man from the sea spoke with undisturbed authority. "Although there other and difficult concepts come in. Repentance, penance, expiation——"

"But that's not how my mind works."

"Isn't it? It's not always easy to be sure. But I think I know the ideas your mind does feed on. Cheapness, humiliation, disgrace."

"Nothing of the sort." Cranston was impatient. He had found the cigarettes and was about to light one. But before he could strike a match, something further burst from him. "The dishonour!"

The man from the sea had been fumbling for the cigarette packet in his turn. But at this he stopped and was strangely still. "Dishonour?" he asked unemotionally. "It's the same as disgrace, isn't it?"

"No."

The man from the sea laughed—but his laughter had no effect upon an indefinable sense of crisis that had built itself up in the summer-house. "I should have thought that it was only in rather deeper waters that one learned that."

"What do you know about it?"

"Didn't I come from them—before your eyes? Let me have the matches, will you?"

Cranston pushed the box across the table. "It's dishonour when you have to say *never*. Never, never, never."

"When I was stripping for that swim, I lost my watch. I took it from a pocket, meaning to transfer it to this belt. But I was at the rail, and my hand slipped." The man from the sea paused. "It's a habit it has."

"Your hand?" Cranston was puzzled.

"Never mind. That's another story. My hand slipped, I say—and the watch had vanished in an instant. Honour —dishonour: is that how you see them?"

"Yes. Never, never, never. . . . You are going to say one can dive."

"I am. But—my dear boy—it has to be to the very bottom of the deep. . . . My eyes are still smarting like the devil, but I don't see that I need deny myself a cigarette."

There was a moment's silence in the summer-house, and somewhere in the distance Cranston heard a cock crow. Sally had been longer than she reckoned. He tried to remember the time of the single early-morning train down the branch line. Then, at the spurt of the match, he glanced at his companion. The small intense flame lit up the face of the man from the sea. It was evident that he

55

could see nothing. But his attitude was of one glancing downward. Once already—but less clearly—Cranston had glimpsed him in that pose, and had felt his memory obscurely stir. It stirred again now—and to such an effect that he cried out.

The man from the sea raised his head. His eyes, horribly bloodshot and almost closed, were directed for a moment sightlessly before him. And then he blew out the match. "Did you speak?" he said.

"I know you." Cranston took a deep breath. "You're Day."

CHAPTER V

"Yes—I'm Day." The man from the sea struck another match and lit his cigarette. "But we never met before to-night?"

"Photographs. There were no end of photographs when—when it happened. No wonder you know about Alex Blair—and remembered meeting his wife at some grand scientific do."

"If you recognise me from a photograph, other people will be capable of doing the same thing. It's part of my problem, as you can guess."

"No doubt." Cranston had gone to the door of the summer-house and was peering into the garden, the nearer outlines of which were becoming faintly visible. "As I now know that you're John Day I'd better say that my name is Richard Cranston. But it's not a very equal exchange of information." He swung round. "What made you do it?"

"Go—or come back?" The man called John Day got to his feet, and as he did so put both hands across his eyes. "Curse this stuff! Has something gone wrong, do you think? The girl ought to be back by now."

"I think she ought. But we can give her a few more minutes before worrying."

"And go on talking? Now, what was it about? Honour and dishonour, I think—and diving to the very bottom of the deep. That's why I've come back. It's my dive. As for why I went—well, I believe people have written books about it."

Cranston was silent. The dimensions of what he was involved with were coming home to him. When John Day had taken a holiday in Switzerland, vanished, been glimpsed in Vienna and vanished again, Cranston had still been at school. He remembered hysterical stuff in newspapers. And he remembered his senior physics master, uncommunicative but grim. Two years later there had been a particular sort of explosion in the heart of the Asiatic land-mass. Instruments in North Africa, in California, in New South Wales had recorded it. One man's deciding to differ from his immediate fellows could mean that—could even sway the balance, perhaps, in which hung the fate of nations. And now here was John Day in the Blairs' summer-house. He had just conducted a good-humoured inquisition into the momentous matter of a young man's having developed a morbid sense of guilt in consequence of mucking a love-affair.

Day had found his way across the summer-house and was fingering—like the blind man that he momentarily was—the heap of clothes which Sally had left on a bench. "Let me be quite plain," he said, "that what I called a moment ago my problem is a purely practical one. The larger issues, you see, I have got entirely clear."

"Was the solution as simple as you say mine is—as simple as a right-about turn? Is that what you're doing—turning?"

"Turning my coat again, I think you mean? I suppose it might be put that way."

"You have plans?"

"I have a very simple plan."

"But not so simple that you don't require help?"

"It's possible that I need only a bowl of water—in addition, that is, to what are clearly these admirable clothes. If I can get rid of this sand and reasonably see——" Day broke off—and a moment later uttered in a strange voice a single word. "Harris!"

"What's that?" Cranston was startled.

"This jacket—or whatever it is. Harris tweed. I suddenly got the smell of it—and smell's a damned queer thing. It's four years since I've had decent—since I've had western clothes in my hands. Clothes are damned queer too, by the way."

Cranston made no reply. Sally's delay was disturbing, but nevertheless he hoped now that it would last a little longer. If he said nothing Day might fall silent—and then he could think. He desperately needed to. He was aware that some great responsibility had descended upon him, and that he must put himself the right questions and find himself the right answers. When Day—as a mere unknown—had come a fugitive from the sea Cranston had prided himself on finding one right answer at once. In his own private affairs he had guessed very badly— had behaved very badly. He had been becoming aware of it. And the ability suddenly to decide rightly about the fugitive—to acknowledge that he must be given simple human solidarity until he had a chance to declare and explain himself: this ability had brought him its odd comfort for a time. But how was he to act now—suddenly caught up by the necessity not for some merely private decision but for a decision very conceivably involving vast public issues?

His first duty was to remember his years. He saw this at once—and felt a faint flicker of intellectual satisfaction, of intellectual pride, in so seeing it. At least he still had a clear head. There was a sense in which he had the largest confidence in himself, and of this not even his having so mucked things could substantially rob him. But at the same time he knew that here was something which he ought not to be taking on alone. He paused on this. Where did such an acknowledgement lead? Ought he to leave the summer-house, affecting perhaps to search for Sally, and go straight to the house and rouse Alex Blair? And, if he turned this suggestion down, ought he not to be very sure that his reason for doing so had nothing to do with the privately disastrous disclosures that would almost certainly follow?

For a moment it seemed to him that here *was* the obvious course. Blair was the nearest person of standing and of mature judgment. More than this, he was himself an eminent scientist, already knowing something of Day both as a man and as a physicist.

Cranston extinguished his cigarette and walked out to the verandah. Day did nothing to stop him. The sky was faintly luminous and there was a bar of orange in the east. He fancied that he heard peewits crying very far away. He couldn't go to the house. Abruptly he knew this absolutely. But he was unable to find the reason. Only he thought it wasn't funk about Caryl. He turned back into the summer-house and found that there was at least a line of enquiry in his head. "The police," he said boldly. "This must mean the police for you, sooner or later. Why not now?"

"The police? No. They're no part of my plan."

"I don't understand you. You've come back as the only way of—of recovering your watch. You can't expect a reception by the Lord Mayor of London. And if you really believe that the fellow off the ship will presently be raising a whole hunt against you—well, I'd have thought you might as well get yourself safely locked up sooner rather than later."

"You'd like me safely locked up?"

"I can't be sure about you. Suppose your eyes clear up with a little bathing, and you are able to get along by yourself. Ought I just to let you disappear? Oughtn't I to be more—more suspicious of you than that? You left this country meaning mischief to it, and it seems very possible that you've come back to it meaning more. If it isn't your intention to contact the authorities, oughtn't I to be very suspicious of your story indeed? If you can be said to have produced a story at all."

"You'd like to listen to the confessions of a penitent traitor? My Life of Disillusionment behind the Iron Curtain—that sort of thing?"

"Not that. But you mayn't be at all as you represent yourself. For instance, it seems very queer that you should just arrive like this. I don't see how you can have done it. You must have been quite tremendously a marked man— watched and guarded right round the clock. How on earth could you have smuggled yourself on a ship due to skirt the Scottish coast?"

"I couldn't—and I didn't. I wasn't any sort of a stowaway, my dear chap. I was the star turn on board. We were on a little scientific cruise."

"Scientific?" Cranston reached for another cigarette. "You mean some sort of deviltry?"

"Just that. You can guess the sort of thing." Day was ironic. "Call it doing something sinister to the Gulf Stream. Or perhaps the Sargasso Sea."

"Rubbish."

"Quite so. Still, the motive of our cruise was simple enough. Forty years ago its equivalent would have been, say, charting the other fellow's mine-fields. Nowadays one noses out other things, and the job requires far higher technical skill. Not that I didn't have the deuce of a time getting the assignment."

"Because you were any number of cuts above it?"

"Just that. But I persuaded them that I had a valuable and intimate knowledge of the terrain. So

61

they sent me. And then they let me slip. You are still sceptical?"

"I don't know that I can be—just about that. What I came in on didn't look like a put-up show. But wasn't it pretty feeble of them?"

"Perhaps so. But it was outside their expectations, outside their very comprehensive system of suspicions. An act of sudden individual initiative, proceeding from an entirely private and personal—what shall we call it?— movement of the spirit. It's what sometimes takes people their way, you may say. But they're slow to realise that it can be a two-way traffic."

"What did your movement of the spirit prompt you to stuff in that belt?" Cranston paused—and thought that he sensed Day stiffen. "The inner secrets of the Kremlin? Chats on nuclear physics?"

"Money—dollars and francs and pounds sterling." Day's familiar laugh was at its easiest. "In quite astonishingly large amounts—which I had the devil of a job getting together. If you care to hit me on the head and bury me in the garden, you can set yourself up on the proceeds handsomely."

For a moment Cranston said nothing, and the ugly little joke hung in air. "Money?" he asked presently. "Do your simple plans need such a lot of it? You'll have free keep in Pentonville or Brixton." There was a further silence, and he realised that this, too, had been ugly enough. "I just want to make sense of you," he said.

"I hadn't much idea, you see, where my break-away might happen. Or who might have to be bribed to do what. I envisaged a great many possibilities. Science, you know, trains one to that sort of thinking ahead."

"It doesn't seem to have trained you to think sufficiently ahead in the first instance."

"We can all get things wrong."

They were back, Cranston felt, where they had started. He went again to the door and listened. Sally's absence was now alarming. He turned round. "It would be easier, wouldn't it, if you could bribe me?"

"Very much easier." Day spoke whimsically. "But of course you are incorruptible—in matters of this sort. And I don't think you are to be blackmailed either— which is a suggestion I rather carelessly made to you. It is awkward about Lady Blair and so on. But it would no longer count with you."

"It certainly wouldn't. Not now that I know who you are."

"But what does still count is the fact that we've both mucked it. My chance seems to be to trade on that." The words came softly to Cranston with the effect of cards dropped deliberately on a table. "Each of us has let himself down." Day broke off. "Surely it's growing light? What's the time?"

"Dawn is certainly coming. But I can't tell you the time. I haven't—— "

"You haven't got a watch either. And your word for the condition is the precise one. Dishonour. And, just because you have let yourself down, you won't now let me down—until you're certain that I'm no good. Until you're certain that my deep, deep dive is bogus. Isn't it queer? Isn't it extraordinary that, staggering at random from the sea, I should run straight into a full-blown young romantic idealist?"

"She's coming!" Cranston had moved swiftly to the door. Now he was back again. "Can't you speak out— straight? What are you going to do? What's this plan you talk about?"

It was perhaps because Sally's footsteps could already

63

be heard on the path that Day replied in the softest voice he had yet used. "I've told you that my plan is very simple. It's the simplest of all plans."

"The simplest——?"

"Ssh!"

CHAPTER VI

THE GIRL was in the doorway. She carried a bowl and a
large jug, and there was a basket over her arm. "It's no
good," she said, "trying to beat the dawn at this time of
year."

Cranston took the jug from her. "As a matter of fact,
you've been rather a long time. It wasn't . . . your
mother again?"

"I've no doubt Mother is asleep—ankle and all." Sally
put down the bowl and basket composedly. "Alex."

"Alex!" He was startled.

"I thought your friend would at least be dressed." She
turned to Day. "You're not a doctor—or anything like
that? You have no special knowledge of what to do? The
water's warm, and with boracic. I'd simply try opening
your eyes in it. And I've brought some of the dark stuff—
argyrol, isn't it?—and a dropper. Will you come over
here?"

She was as impersonal as a nurse, and Day submitted to
her. Cranston watched from a corner. There was still no
more than a pale grey light in the summer-house, but
objects and actions could be distinguished. Certainly there
could now be no question of getting away under cover of
any approximation to darkness.

"Sally," he said, "you mean that Sir Alex knows?"

"Knows what, Dick?"

The cool question seemed to him like a flash of lightning
on what Sally herself must now know. But he went
through with answering steadily. "About this chap—and
what we're up to."

65

"I'll empty out this water. And then you can try again. Do you want a towel?" Sally made various dispositions at the table before she turned again to Cranston. "I'd just got into the house when there was—Alex. He was up and prowling. I can't think why."

"The shots, perhaps. If he heard them he'd know at once it wasn't aircraft practising."

"No doubt. It was awkward."

"I'm frightfully sorry, Sally."

"Really?" For a second she was rather coldly mocking. "It was one of those occasions on which one has to risk a great deal of the truth in order not to give away the whole of it."

There was a little silence. The words, quietly uttered in the fresh young voice, seemed to hang oddly in the air. It was Day who spoke. "Did you feel that you had so much truth at your disposal?"

She made no reply to this. It was as if she was determined to have only the most businesslike relations with him. Instead she turned again to Cranston. "I told him that it was you—here in the summer-house, Dick. I told him that you had wakened me by throwing gravel at my window, and that it was a question of some poaching exploit gone wrong. You and a friend had been guddling Lord Urquhart's trout—and had lost nearly all your clothes and come by a great many scratches. Of course I'm sorry to have represented you in rather a juvenile light. You're the last person I'd really think of as—getting into mischief. But I had to consider what would amuse Alex— amuse him without really interesting him. I gather you don't want him out here."

"I don't think we do."

"If he does come out it will be in the most good-natured way in the world—a matter of what he calls

66

jollying you up." She spoke with her flicker of fastidious disdain. "But you can bank on his laziness, no doubt."

Day raised his head from the big bowl. "Is Sir Alex Blair so very lazy?"

"If he weren't wealthy and lazy he'd be in the very top flight of British scientists to-day. And he knows it, I imagine." Her voice was indifferent. "Has all this helped?"

"It has made me much more comfortable. But I still can't really see."

"Hadn't we better get a doctor?"

Day shook his head. "My guess is that time, and only time, will clear it up. A doctor would do no more than produce reassuring talk and a roll of bandages."

"I haven't any talk. But I can produce dark glasses. I slipped some into the basket. Also a flask of brandy, a packet of biscuits and a block of chocolate. And, Dick, here's the pullover. Canary, I'm afraid—but it won't go too badly with your tan. I shall go in now—and leave you to evolve whatever further adventure you have a mind to."

She was gone—before Cranston could speak. But he strode after her and caught her on the verandah. "Sally——" He broke off, confused and finding himself without words.

They were facing each other. He had a sense that—inexplicably—she was trembling all over. But for the moment they stood confronted, her gaze at least was perfectly steady. "I know how you feel," she said. "At least . . . I know how you feel."

She had turned, run down the little flight of steps, and was hurrying through the dimness of the garden. He found himself repeating the banal words as if they had come to him charged with impenetrable mystery.

67

"A capable girl." Day was opening the brandy flask.
"Yes."

"Knows just what she is about."

For a moment Cranston was silent. These last words—
he strangely and intuitively knew—were not true. Perhaps
Day was deceived. But Day was a liar. He had to remember that. All the stuff about diamonds: the fellow
would have persisted in it if there had been a chance of
sustaining that particular deception. . . . "Shall we get
back to business?" Cranston asked.

"Brandy, biscuits and chocolate are decidedly part of
our business at present. Would you pour out? It's a thing
the blind find tricky." Day paused only for a moment.
"Do you play rugger?"

"Yes." Cranston poured—and drank.

"Three-quarter?"

"Yes. But I don't see——"

"That we're getting back to business? But we are, you
know. You had fumbled a pass. How unforgivably, you
were just coming to realise. And you remember the next
stage? An absolute determination to take the ball cleanly
next time. Well—I'm the ball. I think that was about as
far as we had got."

"And I think you've laboured all that long enough.
I'm prepared to admit that it's not precisely nonsense.
But taking the ball cleanly mayn't at all mean anything
that you greatly fancy." Cranston reached for a biscuit
and paused to munch it. "Your story may be full of
psychological interest. Your wanderings—physical and
spiritual—among the nations may open up all sorts of
fascinating vistas upon the dilemma of modern man.
Everything of that sort. High-class thriller stuff, in which
recurrent chapters are devoted to an anatomy of the
soul." The small swig of brandy, Cranston realised, had

gone straight to his head. "But the fact remains that you are almost certainly even more dangerous than you are interesting. Taking *you* cleanly ought perhaps to mean putting you inside as fast as the job can be done. . . . I've halved the chocolate."

"Thank you—and of course you're right. There's a presumption, I mean, that I'm far too dangerous not to jump on. But suppose it's otherwise. Suppose I can convince you that—well, that all that's over and done with. Suppose you wanted to help me—to go on helping me, I ought to say. Could you do it?"

"Could I help you?" Cranston was disconcerted at being thus abruptly placed once more in the position of the challenged party.

"Just that. For there's not much point in my telling you anything more—opening any of those fascinating vistas you're so neatly ironic about—if in fact your neat undergraduate wit is altogether in excess of your practical capacities. I'll admit you cut a pretty good figure, my dear young man, in the matter of the fellow with the gun. But are you resourceful? And are you your own master at present from day to day? Could you get a blinded man from here to London—perhaps against desperate opposition? There's more to a good wing-three-quarter, you'll agree, than just taking the ball cleanly. He has to carry it over the line."

"I think you have the most frightful cheek." Reduced to this rather juvenile sentiment, Cranston picked up another square of chocolate. Brandy, he had decided, was an unsuitable sort of refreshment at dawn.

"Alex Blair, I take it, is the grand person hereabouts—the laird, and all that. We're now in the grounds of the big house."

"It's a castle, as a matter of fact—Dinwiddie Castle.

And I'm not sure that 'laird' is quite grand enough for our host. Not that he wouldn't be perfectly pleased with it."

"And you? It's plain that you are on terms of intimacy —varying degrees of intimacy, shall we say?—with the grand folk. But who are you? And where do you come from?"

"I'm the doctor's son—and from three miles away. But my parents are very respectable." No doubt because of the brandy, Cranston was unable to refrain from further sarcasm. "Our family connections are, if anything, superior to the Blairs'. So if you're wondering if I qualify for your——"

"And you can come and go as you please during your holidays—your vacation? You can go home this morning and simply announce that you will be away for a week?"

Cranston flushed. "Of course I can."

"Borrowing a car?"

"I've got a car."

"But this is capital." Day took another biscuit. "You are decidedly worth converting."

"To those plans?"

"Precisely."

"The plans that you say are so simple?"

"My dear young man—yes, indeed. My plans *are* very simple. I am going to die."

For a moment the small, bleak statement held the air unchallenged. Then, from somewhere far down the garden, a dog barked and a man's voice was heard calling. Other dogs joined in. The man's voice rose again—cheerful, commanding, but of no effect amid the clamour of terriers.

"It's Sir Alex." Cranston had no doubts. "He makes a

thorough nuisance of himself at times, I've been told—fooling around long before breakfast with the Cairns."

"He'll come up here?"

"Very probably he will, now that he's in the garden. . . . What do you mean?"

"Just what I say—that quite soon I shall be dead. It's a great simplification of things. . . . But can't we get away?"

"There's nothing behind this summer-house except a high wall and then the cliff. And if we go down the garden we shall simply walk into him. But need you worry? It must be a simplification in the matter of new acquaintances too. If you are going to be dead, I mean, virtually before you need return Sir Alex's call."

Day laughed—but low and cautiously. "I see you don't believe me—yet."

"How do you know I don't believe you?"

"You wouldn't make just that joke. Your feelings, you know, are at present superior to your morals."

"Will he recognise you?"

"What's the light like? I get the impression of clear daylight."

"It's pretty well that."

"Then I suppose he will."

They were now whispering. The voice in the garden was raised in song, and the Cairns were responding with a more frenzied yapping. Cranston moved to the door of the summer-house. "I'm sure Sally did her best," he said. "But she over-estimated his laziness and under-estimated his curiosity."

"Not, with most scientists, an easy thing to do." Day, Cranston saw, had got to his feet and was contriving to peer painfully about the table. "Didn't she say something about dark glasses? Ah—here they are."

The singing was quite close, and the terriers could be heard scampering. Sir Alex Blair's voice broke off in the middle of a stave and then raised itself again in robust speech. No doubt it was what Sally had called his jollying manner. "Dick, my boy, come out and declare yourself! Don't forget that I'm a magistrate, sir. Come out, I say, or I'll send the hounds in."

Day slipped on the glasses. "The question," he murmured "was of your resourcefulness. Say, the quickness of your wit."

Cranston turned and walked out to the verandah. It was outrageous that he should be thus challenged. He moved to the top of the steps, and as he did so ran a hand through his hair. The gesture told him at once that he was on a stage. It went with an engaging grin. "Hullo, Sir Alex," he called. "Did Sally peach?"

"She had no choice, poor wretch. I caught her red-handed." Blair had at least come to a halt. Clipped and brushed and polished, florid and well-dieted, dressed in a faded kilt and carrying the shepherd's crook he commonly affected when at Dinwiddie, he was glancing up at Cranston, facetiously severe. "And you too, you young scoundrel—what have you to say for yourself?"

"Nothing at all, Sir Alex. As usual—nothing at all."

"And so I'd suppose. Still—deeds sometimes speak louder than words—eh? What have you brought me for breakfast, my boy? What have you brought the corrupt old capon-justice of Dinwiddie?"

Cranston grinned—and for good measure again put on the turn with his hair. "I'm sorry to say, sir, we didn't get a single fish. They were on top of us far too quickly."

"Not a single one of Urquhart's trout?" This time Sir Alex's severity appeared genuine. "I wouldn't have thought it of you, Dick—I wouldn't indeed. And what's

72

this about the other fellow having to cut and run without his clothes? Guddling for grilse in the deep pools, eh?"

"It was pretty bad, sir—a thorough rout of the anti-Urquhart forces. The less said about it the better."

"Very well, very well—I'll leave you both to your shame. If you recover face in time, join us at breakfast." Turning away, Sir Alex fell to whistling up his dogs. Then he turned back. "But—just in case you don't—I'll come up and be introduced to the chap now. Only civil, eh?"

"Steady on, sir." Cranston discreetly lowered his voice. "Aren't you taking something for granted?"

"What's that, Dick? What d'you mean?"

"Well, sir, about it's being . . . a chap."

Sir Alex stared. "But Sally said——"

"I'm sure Sally would say the right thing, sir."

"Well, I'm damned!" Sir Alex lowered his voice. "One of those madcap McGilvrays—eh, Dick?"

"Tales out of school, sir."

"Quite right, quite right. You may rely on me, my dear fellow." Sir Alex dropped his voice to a robust whisper. "And left in her pelt . . .? You young dog!" He burst into a loud guffaw, checked himself, and turned away with a quick wave. "Come over and see us soon, my boy. Sally likes it."

Cranston watched his retreat down the garden. Once more he had been obliged to choose. And he had chosen instinctively. He knew that he could have taken no other course. He knew too that it had been, this time, a real burning of his boats. Sir Alex represented the established order of things. He was, as he had humourously remarked, a magistrate—and much else besides. And Cranston had stood on his verandah and lied to him. He had lied to him by way of concealing and protecting John Day.

He turned back into the summer-house. It was still

shadowy there, and for a moment he distinguished little after the clear morning light. And then he saw that Day had sat down again at the table. He was oddly posed, with his hands stretched out before him, palm upwards. Cranston took a couple of steps towards him and stopped. He found himself staring at the palm of Day's right hand. And Day knew what he was doing. "Look closer," he said —and after a pause: "You've never seen anything like that?"

"No—I haven't." Cranston felt an uncertain sensation in his stomach. "Is it . . . important? I'm not a—a pathologist."

Day closed his fist. "I think I mentioned—didn't I?—a bad habit of mine?"

"About your hand slipping?"

"Yes. This is something that began happening when my hand slipped—not very long ago. It was then, you know, that I decided to come . . . home."

CHAPTER VII

"It's how you know you're going to——?" Cranston hesitated.

"Yes. It's as certain as the tokens that used to tell people about the plague. Interesting, don't you think? Your father would be fascinated. And lucky, too—if he could get hold of me. A unique case, you know. Nothing like me in these islands to-day. Of course, in Japan——"

Day, who had followed Cranston back to the verandah, broke off to stretch himself lazily in the morning warmth that already seemed to be breaking over the garden like a wave. It was a gesture, the young man realised with a shiver, of simple luxury in the sense of being alive. But Day's tone continued ironical. "Would you be inclined," he asked, "to see in it the operation of what they used to call poetic justice?"

"No." Cranston put out a hand and guided his companion to a seat on the steps. Then he sat down beside him. They might have been two friends on some idle holiday, lucky in the weather, and up at sunrise with no very definite plan in their heads. "It doesn't prompt me to any fancy thoughts at all. Or even"—he was awkward—"to say anything much."

"Then tell me about the view."

"The view? Well, there's a screen of pine trees beyond the garden, and one just gets a glimpse of the battlements and turrets of the castle."

"It's a real castle?"

"Basically. But it's been cobbled up a great deal, and a lot of Abbotsford Gothic added on. The main turret is quite bogus. Incidentally, there's a flag being broken from it now. Blair is a great stickler for that sort of thing. He inherited unexpectedly, you know, when he was a professor of physics in some dim university."

"Do you notice the scents?" For a moment Day had been inattentive. "They're changing. They're no longer those of the night. I suppose it's the sort of thing one becomes sensitive to when really blind." He paused. "Any other sights?"

"The flag is just fluttering. That means there's a light breeze blowing off-shore. And dead above it—I mean what looks dead above it—there's a kestrel hovering. . . . Is it really—just that?"

"Just——?"

Cranston glanced almost furtively at Day. He was still stripped—experiment with Sir Alex Blair's clothes was something he appeared willing to defer—and his spare body showed itself in clear daylight as much an athlete's as it had done when glinting beneath the moon.

"Is it really true that—that you have come home like a sick animal——?"

"To die in my own hole? Perhaps it is—a little. But chiefly I want to see my wife." Day's voice had gone suddenly expressionless. "And sons."

There was a long silence. It might all be lies. And if it was true, then its background was an experience upon which Cranston could have no proper comment at all. Yet it seemed wrong not to say something—and something as directly relevant as he could reach to. "Are you sure," he asked, "that they want to see you?"

"I don't suppose they do. But I want to apologise. It was rough on them, you know . . . my doing what I did."

"Thoughtless?" Cranston asked the question with what he felt as a sudden irrepressible enormous irony of his own.

76

"Yes."

Day's voice was again utterly without expression. It occurred to Cranston to wonder whether his experiences —or perhaps the first working inward of his mortal malady—had unhinged his mind. "You'll feel better," he asked, "when forgiven, and assured that by-gones are by-gones?"

"Nothing like that. Don't you remember? *Never.* Never, never, never."

"But you have had to come, all the same?"

Day answered obliquely. "It was difficult to do."

"The escaping?"

"Yes—and leaving my work. Particularly with only a few more months chance of it."

Cranston had an impulse to jump up and run for the castle—the impulse of a small child venturesomely bathing, who suddenly knows that the next breaker may go over his head. "You don't make things any easier," he managed to say. "You don't make it at all clear where you now stand."

"Not on any particularly rational ground." Day had put on the dark glasses, and as he turned his head towards Cranston he had the appearance of scrutinising him seriously. "To come back—through difficulties, as I've said—and tell her that I had been wrong: well, it has seemed the only thing to do."

"Wrong, as they say, ideologically? You've lost faith in——?"

"Not particularly." Day's voice was indifferent. "But then I don't know that, particularly, I ever had it."

"Then why——?"

"I wanted recognition, facilities, a different sort of sense of power." Day's voice was suddenly vibrant. "To run my own show. To be clean at the top."

77

"And by going over to them you got there?"

"No." With what Cranston obscurely sensed to be an immense effort of will, Day spoke flatly again. "I got higher. But not right up."

"Surely you might have guessed as much at the start?"

"Yes, indeed." Day was now blandly acquiescent, persuasive. "I was rationalising, no doubt. Indeed, eventually I proved it to myself. I got at a deeper motive—by a sort of auto-analysis. Chiefly, it all had to do with my father."

"Your father?"

"He died when I was twelve—but he remained my great problem, all the same. Acute father-eclipse. That, basically, was what sent me to Russia."

"I suppose that's Freud or somebody? I had a notion your late friends don't much go in for that sort of mythology."

Day shook his head. "No more they do. I had to get it all out of books. And that was partly what made working out the whole thing so difficult. But I got it clear in the end."

"I see." Cranston utttered the words mechanically. For it seemed to him that this was flabby talk, not easily to be reconciled either with that desperate swim or with what he continued to sense of concentrated purpose in the man before him. "It all comes to you as a private matter?"

"Absolutely. That is where the only real treacheries lie—in the sphere of personal relations. That is where dishonour comes. Don't you know it?"

Cranston was silent—somewhat in the fashion that he was silent at home when his father or mother made what he thought of as a completely "period" remark. There was nothing that could usefully be said. But he might ask one further probing question. "You feel that your slip-up was in the shame and so-forth you brought on your wife and children? It's a social response to your action that has made you regret it, and not the emergence of a conviction that it was inherently wrong in itself?"

"How charming is divine philosophy." Day was suddenly mocking. "And catching, too. Didn't your tutor think up questions like that?"

Cranston stood up. "You can't escape—a person with your history can't escape—having a public self. And it's the only self the world at large is going to bother about. You're the man who has carried enormously valuable information, I suppose, to a potential enemy. And now you've turned up out of the sea, disposed to conversation about your wife and children. It may be true that nothing now seems important to you except getting square with them—except making some sort of symbolic gesture to them and then packing up. But it can be done in gaol. I believe they arrange these things decently enough nowadays. And why shouldn't you accept that? If what you say about—about your health is true, then it's no more than an extra penny for you to pay. . . . And there's another thing——"

"I hope there are several." Day smiled, and the smile seemed less artificial than his laughter had done. "Do you know, you make me a little wonder if I'm off my head? And you intoxicate me, too."

"Intoxicate you?" Cranston was disconcerted.

"You see, you're the first person for a very long time to whom I've talked anything but physics or political claptrap. Imagine, my dear chap, spending your life in a lab— certainly a splendid lab—and leaving it only for an eternal Rotarian lunch or Primrose League tea-party. Think how delightful, after that, a nice lad from Cambridge must be." Day paused. "But I interrupted you."

"I say there's another thing. What you carried in one direction, you are now carrying back—and with interest, I don't doubt—in the other. Willynilly you are doing that, since the stuff must all be there in your head. I believe everything you say now about the chap who came at us with that gun. He's rousing every fellow-spy in the country. And that ship is sending out coded signals like billyho. And here you are, stranded and helpless in Scotland, with no resources but a nice lad from Cambridge—if you can catch him." Cranston allowed himself to pause briefly on this shaft. "Hours are slipping by—and you're getting nowhere. But those people certainly are. It seems to me that if you want that meeting with your wife—and I don't pretend to comment on it or on what it means to you—your only real chance of it is to send me to find a copper. Or Blair. He'll call out a territorial regiment, or raise the clan if you've a fancy for it. That's where security lies—not in a crazy dash for London."

"*Your* security?"

Cranston felt himself flush. "Yes, damn it—*my* security. And my country's, if that's not something too unimportant to mention."

"It's a reasonable point of view—at least in a layman. But one of the troubles, you know, of my line of business is the melodramatic light in which the public is inclined to regard it. Still, I wish I could fall in with your plan. Unfortunately it wouldn't be at all the same thing. My wife coming and taking a peep at me—no doubt after having my arrival and arrest tactfully broken to her by a smooth old person from the Home Office? No, no—it's just not what I see."

"Isn't what you see itself a bit of melodrama—and not perhaps very considerate of the other people involved?

The essence of it is walking in—just freely walking in—on your family?"

Day nodded. "Yes. Is it very queer? It may be—as I've said—that I'm a bit off my head. On the other hand, it might seem less queer—mightn't it—to somebody——"

"Less immature and inexperienced and so forth than myself?" Cranston took this up quite seriously. "I suppose so. And yet it isn't just a blank to me. You are telling me about a sort of *idée fixe*. And I can see a person in your situation genuinely having it. There isn't *really* any return to that domestic past of yours. It's a matter of never-never-never, all right. And so there is only this gesture. It doesn't at all make nonsense to me. But whether it's genuine in *you* remains rather an open question." Cranston rose. "I'll think about it as I walk home."

"That's what you're going to do?"

"Yes. You'll be all right here—and conversely, I don't see that you can take matters much into your own hands at present. And I'll be back."

"With your mind made up?" Day, too, got to his feet. "Very well. But perhaps you'll give me a hand into some of those clothes before you go."

"Certainly." Cranston moved back into the summer-house. "Not that you're likely to have visitors."

"You don't think Blair will come back?"

Cranston shook his head. "I'm pretty sure he will keep tactfully away—and tactfully mum. He really does believe that I've been fooling around with some——" Cranston broke off, confused.

"With some madcap girl from among your neighbours—whereas it was really with his wife?" Day might have been offering this in a spirit of mild humour. "And he isn't even wondering whether he's been told a lie."

It came as an enormous relief to be alone, and half-way down the garden Cranston stopped and took a deep breath. There was a large tumbling shrub of damask roses beside him; he put his head right into it and took a deep breath of that too. It was like the action of a man escaped from a charnel-house, and it told him how vivid his sense of John Day's condition had been. The man was really carrying his death about with him: there was no question—Cranston seemed to know it instinctively—of a lie there. And yet the horror of it did not mean that Day repelled him. When he had helped the blinded man to dress he had felt no trace of bodily revulsion. The simple physical sympathy that had established itself when Day had come lurching out of the sea and they had instantly gone into hiding together still existed. It was in itself something altogether unremarkable, and yet Cranston knew that in his present strange situation it counted for a great deal. It helped on—that was it—the insidious and surely wholly irrational sense of identification with Day which a rather sketchy correspondance in their situations had given birth to. Cranston frowned and walked on. The question was whether he would let Day down.

Or was it? If he allowed himself to put it that way, could there be more than one answer? Must he not acknowledge that he was indeed romantic—or, in a more modern and less flattering idiom, that he was some sort of compulsion-neurotic in the making? Probably he wasn't fit for the sort of experience that Caryl Blair had brought him—and certainly wasn't fit for such experience with a married woman. All that he got out of it—or all that he got out of it except on the most short-term basis—was a pathologically devious sense of guilt. And just when that had been about to break the surface of his consciousness Day had walked up out of the sea. So what had happened was perfectly clear. He had instantly identified himself with one whose occasions were patently unlawful. And then had come a revelation exquisitely calculated to tune up to its very maximum of driving-power this bizarre mechanism of the mind. From the point of view of society Day's guilt had revealed itself as enormous; there was enough of it to satisfy the more inordinate demand for self-punishment. That—Cranston told himself as he halted before the door in the garden wall—that was the way the machine ticked; that was what gave him his large vague sense of implication with the man from the sea. And probably it was a quirk of the mind that grew on one, became obsessive, ended in a total divorce from sober reality. His only chance was to cut out of it at once. He could, at a pinch, tell the whole story to his father. And yet were things so desperate? Could any mind so clever as his own—so swiftly lucid as this admirable piece of self-analysis showed it to be—stand in any substantial danger?

Asking himself this, Cranston opened the door in the high wall and took a step outside. As he did so—as he cast no more than an absent eye on a scene which should have been wholly untenanted—the whole airy fabric of his painful yet intellectually satisfactory ruminations vanished in an instant. In their place stood objective reality—in the person of the man with the trilby hat.

Cranston stepped backwards and softly closed the door. He was almost certain that he had not been seen. The man was standing within a few paces, but his head had been half turned away.

There were two stout bolts on the door. They looked terribly rusty, but it was possible that if cautiously handled they could be fairly silently pushed home. He had no reason to suppose that the man with the trilby hat had managed to arm himself again. But the possibility had to be faced. Had he picked up in an outhouse as much as a pruning-knife or a sickle he would be formidable. Or even a hammer. A hammer or a sickle. . . . Cranston checked himself and got to work on the first bolt. It slid into place with scarcely a creak. The second was more difficult. As he eased it forward he felt sweat upon his forehead. It astonished him that this fresh encounter with the enemy should so key him up. He supposed it was once more a matter of delayed reaction. He hadn't liked that gun. Perhaps he wasn't made for gun-play any more than for——

A faint sound behind him made him whirl round, taut and trembling. It was Sally. She had approached to within a few feet of him and was looking at him in cool astonishment. He suddenly felt a fool. But he kept a sufficient sense of the reality of the situation to raise a finger swiftly to his lips. Then he turned back to the bolt. When satisfied that it was secure he straightened up, beckoned, and walked off down the garden. Sally followed. From the instant of his making his gesture she had been very quiet. He walked far down the garden, but to a point from which he could command a view of most of the wall he had just left. Then he stopped. "It's the chap who had the gun," he said. "He's hanging around."

"This is something you've got mixed up with quite by chance?"

"Yes."

"And that you haven't really got the hang of?"

"I've got a good deal of it now." Cranston looked at Sally cautiously. She must have returned to the garden for the purpose of talking to him again, but now she had an air of waiting for him to take some initiative. "It's very queer."

"You seem to have thrown Alex off the scent. But isn't it a little hard on whichever of the McGilvray girls he——?"

"That was simply a conclusion he jumped at. I didn't mean to put into his head any particular—particular girl."

"I'm sure you are thoroughly thoughtful of female reputations."

She had forced herself, he felt, to come out with this hard stroke. And now she had gone pale and her eyes were on the ground. He felt desperate. "Look," he said, "it's no good pretending. I know it's all been too rotten——"

"All?" She seemed strangely startled—even frightened. And then she was cold again. "Don't let's start on heaven knows what. Isn't this man of yours enough to be going on with? And he seems to be on our hands as well as yours. What does the other man want to do? Kill him? Carry him off?" Sally paused. "And who or what is he, anyway? Do you know *that* yet?"

"He's John Day."

Cranston had spoken on impulse, but vehemently. And it seemed to be the intensity of his words, not their content, that surprised her. "Day?" She shook her head. "Somebody well known?"

He saw that it meant nothing to her. And he guessed that it was only the skin of her mind that she was contriving to give to this whole aspect of what the ghastly night had produced. But his understanding of her went no farther than this. He had for a moment the sense of some veiled element in their disastrous relationship. "Don't you remember?" he asked. "A scientist who bolted to——"

"Dick!" She had interrupted round-eyed. "He hasn't come here because of . . . Alex?"

"I'm sure he hasn't. It's pure coincidence that he's now hiding in the summer-house of a fellow-scientist. And he hasn't come back to Britain because of that sort of thing at all. He's a dying man. He had an accident with what was, I suppose, some sort of violently radio-active material. He wants to see his wife." Cranston paused. "Or so he says."

She was puzzled. "But surely a man who has gone off like that can't simply——"

"Of course not. He's virtually an outlaw. And the people he's deserted are after him too. That's the explanation of the chap outside. Do you see now that it all makes a sort of crazy sense?"

"I suppose I do."

"Could you guard Day—just for an hour?"

Sally looked at him in astonishment. "I don't know what you mean. I'm not a daft McGilvray."

"I'd only ask somebody I could trust." Cranston hesitated. It occurred to him that she might answer "I might do it for somebody *I* could trust." But she was silent, and he saw that her pallor had given way to a faint flush. "You see," he said, "I am in a way mixed up with him quite a lot. It's because of something I feel." He stopped again, wondering if she could conceivably guess what he was talking about. But that was too tall an order, since he didn't really understand it himself. "You see," he said again, "I've made up my mind to something. I did it the instant I caught another glimpse of that chap outside. I'm going to take Day to London."

"Is that right? Oughtn't you to speak to Alex? He's amazingly . . . enlightened and tolerant."

He shook his head—and wondered at the same time why her words sounded so very little like a testimonial. "I couldn't do that and then ask Sir Alex to back my plan.

He has responsibilities that I don't have. If I miscalculate and am disgraced it doesn't much matter. But you—you people must be kept clear."

For the first time Sally gave a small exclamation as of pain. But her voice was hard again. "No scandal at Dinwiddie?"

Cranston made no direct reply. She was entitled to come out with these cracks. And yet there was something queer about them. "Shall I explain about you guarding him?" he asked. "I want to go and get the car—and at the same time cook up some story for my people at home. I can't be certain of doing it in less than an hour—perhaps longer. And meantime there's this chap outside. I suspect that he's merely guessing that Day has gone to earth somewhere round Dinwiddie. But it's conceivable that he successfully sleuthed after us in the night. Anyway, he's almost certainly awaiting instructions and reinforcements, and is simply keeping an eye on things meanwhile."

"He's very strategically placed." Sally's tone showed that she had been thinking quickly. "The garden wall runs right to the cliff, and in the other direction he can watch the castle road all the time."

Cranston nodded. "That's true. Of course I can get away by going down the cliff on the other side. Arriving back with the car is a different matter. I'll have to think it out. But my point at the moment is that he just might try to climb in. He's lost his gun, but he may have something ugly in the way of a knife. And as Day seems to be really almost blinded for the time being, he couldn't put up much of a show. So could you get a gun, and plant yourself where you could keep an eye on the summerhouse?"

"I can always get a gun. But the garden's an odd place to be found taking it to."

"Perhaps a carrion crow, or something like that?"

"No doubt I can think of a suitable lie." She looked at her watch. "But it probably won't be necessary, and if we hurry we can put the whole thing through before breakfast. But must you go down the cliff—and the awkward way?"

Sally had spoken with sudden unconcealed anxiety, and this was so overwhelming to him that he had to make an effort to answer calmly. "I think it's my best plan. I doubt if that fellow saw me a few minutes ago, and his suspicions about Dinwiddie may at present be quite vague. But if he did see me leaving the place he would know at once that he was really hot on the scent."

"Very well. I'll get the gun—my own gun—now, and go straight up the garden with it. You needn't waste time after that. Get over the wall and down the cliff as soon as you see me. And I'll stick on the job until I know that you're back on it."

He watched her go. She seemed to draw all his vigilance and all his thought after her, so that for the moment the whole violent and actual adventure into which he had been precipitated appeared shadowy and insubstantial when set beside the mere unfulfilled intention which must be the only memorial of his relation with her. And if he had now a little involved her in the doubtful drama of John Day, it was only partly because the momentary logic of the affair had appeared to require it. He was unwilling to let Sally go, and rather than do so he had brought her into the affair as if she was a boy ready for an escapade. It could hardly be maintained that he had assigned her a post of danger, since she could summon both her step-father and his men-servants readily enough at need. But he wondered whether he ought to have done it, all the same. . . .

There she was—so quickly that it almost seemed as if she must have had the gun ready hidden. She gave him a wave and they moved swiftly on converging paths through the garden, so that when he climbed the wall where it gave directly on the cliff she was no more than twenty yards away. He waved to her in turn and allowed himself to drop.

He was on an outcrop of rock. He had remembered the precise spot where the thing could be done. The wall here was in places part of the outer ward of a former castle, and there were points at which it rose sheer from the cliff. This rendered impossible any walking round it on the outer side, nor could a view of it here possibly be commanded by the lurking man with the trilby hat. It was a climb—at least it was decidedly not a walk—down to sea-level, and the state of the tide meant that he could then do a quick scramble along the rocks until he gained the beach. And there he would recover his bicycle and be home before breakfast was on the table.

If he didn't break his neck. . . . It was trickier than he remembered—particularly at the start—and dropping the first thirty feet required absolute concentration. When he had accomplished this he paused and looked upwards. Sally was perched on the wall almost directly above him. She was attending to her job, for he knew it to be a spot from which there was a clear view of the summer-house. But for the moment she was looking down at him. And he could distinguish—it was as if his senses were tuned to some state of hyperaesthesia by his task—the expression on her intent pale face. There was only one way of describing it. Despair.

Despair. . . . It was by quite a long way, he now realised, that this descent was trickier than he had supposed. And perhaps Sally realised it. Perhaps she was convinced that his chance of avoiding disaster in the next few minutes was very small. And perhaps she——

Cranston made a tremendous effort to thrust out of his mind all speculation on how Sally might, after all, care. The surest way to end up pulped and broken on the rock below was to let his mind wander an inch from his business. And perhaps that was the way that a woman—any woman—would look if she saw a man—any man—in what she judged to be mortal peril.

He gave a reassuring wave, examined the state of his gym-shoes and their laces carefully, and started on the next bit of the drop. When he reached the bottom and looked up again it was no longer possible to see Sally. But her image was still vivid to him. He could see that expression still. Almost, he felt that it might haunt him.

CHAPTER VIII

IT WAS THE memory of Sally's pallor, perhaps, that made Cranston find the appearance of the girl hiker so startling. The girl's face was red and shining, and high on her ruck-sack there was sewn some species of red flag. The effect, from a little distance, was alarmingly Janus-like; approached from front or rear, she would equally present an appearance as of the blazing sun. The sun indeed was suggested by everything about her. Her hair and her khaki shorts and shirt were alike bleached by it, and her limbs—which her garments did not much obscure—were burned brown beneath a glint of fine golden hairs. If one put one's nose to her skin and took a good sniff—Cranston supposed—one would know at last just what the sun smells of.

But Cranston had no thought of this experiment. He had come up with her only a couple of hundred yards from his own garden gate, and he would have skimmed past her rapidly enough if she had not turned and given him a hail. She waved a map as she did so, and it was clear that she was seeking directions. Cranston jammed on his brakes and dismounted. It was something he was unable to do very graciously, for he was both in a great hurry and increasingly burdened by a sense of hopeless stupidities past and problematical actions to come. Nevertheless, as he asked whether he could help he summoned up some sort of smile. The girl had the legs of her shorts rolled up to the thigh, like the awful little trollops who scour the country-side on bicycles at week-ends. Moreover, her accent was of neither of the kinds that Cranston had been brought up to regard as socially acceptable. He had remarked this—

and was attempting to square it with the fact that her shoes were sensible and her fingernails unpainted—when the girl spread out her map in a businesslike fashion over his handlebars. "Will you just show me," she said, "about where I am?"

"The village straight ahead of you is Easter Dinwiddie." Cranston put a finger on the map. "And you're just here."

"Thanks a lot." The girl looked up at the sky and then frankly at Cranston, so that he had a sensation of seeing his own features reflected on her shining cheeks. "I suppose," she said, "that it will be another regular cow?"

"I beg your pardon?" He was bewildered—and anxious to push on.

"The day—really hot."

The girl had dropped the rucksack at her feet. He saw that the red flag had a Union Jack and the Southern Cross on it. "I'd have thought," he said, "that you wouldn't mind heat. You're rather my idea of a salamander."

For a moment she looked puzzled, and he was sorry to have said something unintelligible and therefore unmannerly. "I mean——"

"But of course. We're thrice colder than salamanders in my part of the world. Fires of Spain and the line mean nothing to us. But we don't expect to be grilled when we come to Scotland."

"I suppose not." Cranston felt with his left foot for the pedal of his bike. She had squashed him and he could get on. But if salamanders were not mysterious to her, and she could bandy Donne or whoever it was, why had she looked puzzled? Suddenly he realised that it was because she had noticed his pullover and recognised it as not designed for his sex. This annoyed him. "It's certainly going to be hot," he said, and slung himself over his bike. "But you've made an early start."

"I was glad to. I spent the night in rather a hole. Bed and breakfast. But I didn't stop for the second after sampling the first."

"The bed was a regular cow?"

She looked at him quickly, and it was possible to conceive that she had flushed. Then she picked up the rucksack. "You can't," she asked briefly, "tell me where a Dr. Cranston lives?"

"Just down there, on the left. You can see the drive." And with obscure misgiving he added: "My name is Richard Cranston. I come from there."

"Richard!" The young woman's effulgence seemed to increase—as if, so far, she had after all been shining through a light morning mist. "I'm George," she said, and held out her hand.

"How do you do." He was just in time, he decided, by alertly exerting considerable muscular pressure of his own, to avoid having his fingers badly crushed. "We've been wondering when you would turn up."

Again she gave him her quick look, and when she spoke it was with a shade of defensiveness or distrust. "I only wrote to your mother once—and quite vaguely."

"Yes—but even the off-chance of a visitor is something we do a lot of talking about here." Cranston, who did recall his mother recently murmuring about some itinerant Australian cousin, spoke with decent heartiness. He was sure that an antipodean sun-goddess called George was not at all his style, and the girl's arrival at just this moment was going to complicate his getting briskly away from home. Still, he couldn't do other than welcome her. "Come along," he said. "We're both in time for breakfast."

"Beaut!" George slung her rucksack—which was enormous—lightly on her shoulder. Then, seeing him put

93

out a hand for it, she resigned it without comment. "Do you often go for an early morning spin?"

"No."

He had spoken abruptly, and for a few moments they walked in silence. It occurred to him with a sort of surprise that he still had a natural instinct for telling the truth. The last few weeks, indeed, had given him a sharp schooling in lies, but he was subject to constant dangerous relapse. Perhaps he should have assured George that he went out at crack of dawn quite frequently. He glanced at her cautiously. She seemed to be exactly his own six feet, but to possess an even longer stride. They were covering the ground briskly enough—but she had put her hands in the pockets of her shorts and had the appearance of gently strolling. "I don't really know about your family," she said. "But have you got a sister?"

"No, just one brother—and he's in Germany."

"I see. Do you often arrive home early in the morning in your own pants and somebody else's jersey?"

"No—I don't." He was astounded at this casual frankness—the more so because it couldn't be called, in its manner, either flippant or offensive. "I was doing some nocturnal bathing; and various things happened; and I borrowed this when it turned a bit chilly." He increased his own pace. Sooner or later the lies would have to begin. He might be better at them after a solid breakfast. "Is it so very obviously," he asked, "a woman's jersey?"

"Haven't you a nose?" George was amused.

"A nose? Oh—I see." It was true that the scent of some expensive stuff clung to Sally's pullover and that he had failed to be aware of it. "Here we are." They had walked up the short drive and the uncompromising square house was before them. "Do you find Scottish architecture a bit grim?"

"It does rather hit you—on the Border. But up here it rather isn't quite so bleak or you get used to it. Do I walk straight in?"

He nodded. The front door was open and they walked into the square tiled hall. "At least I can smell coffee," he said. "It's something slightly exotic, insisted upon by my father. But everything you see around you is authentic to the region: chocolate-coloured paint, ground glass in as many of the windows as possible, stags' heads, steel engravings depicting striking incidents in sacred history. Do you like it?"

"I like it very much."

George was emphatic, and he realised, without much caring, that she misinterpreted and disliked his tone. Moreover, she seemed suddenly slightly awkward. Perhaps she was afraid of melting something or of setting the whole place on fire. But conceivably the awkwardness was really his own. Leaving things at the castle as he had done, he felt that every minute had to be counted. But he could scarcely now simply scribble a note for his mother, grab a couple of rolls, get out the car and vanish. If only——

He became aware that George was expecting something, and he took an inspired guess at it. Her mind would work in terms of a tradition of unquestioning hospitality. "Look," he said, "nobody seems to be about yet. But you'll want to go to your room. I'll show you."

She nodded and he led the way upstairs. Fortunately there always was a room in decent order. He would shove George into it. And then—it came to that—he would rapidly plan his escape.

His mother was in the kitchen, so he knew there would be scrambled eggs. On this simple dish Mrs. Cranston held strict views, and she seldom allowed it to be prepared by other hands. He had laid a fourth place at the table before she entered the breakfast-room. He kissed her. "The Australian cousin has come," he said. "I was out early and met her. She had slept goodness knows where. I put her in the spare bedroom. She'll be down any minute."

"Then you must have yours boiled." Taking her son's news very much in her stride, Mrs. Cranston turned back to the kitchen. "Elspeth, boil two eggs for Master Richard. And make a little more toast and add one cupful of boiling water to the coffee." She returned to her son. "I felt Georgiana might just turn up. I shall be so pleased to meet her."

"She's not Georgiana. She's George."

"How very amusing! And is she charming?"

"Charming?" It was one of his mother's period tricks to take it for granted that one must develop a sort of moonstruck interest in any fresh girl on the horizon. "She's quite terrible—enormous and roasted and toasted and without a pure vowel in the——"

"You should be ashamed of yourself. She's your father's cousin and she's in my house." Mrs. Cranston could be briskly formidable.

"Yes, I know. And I'm sorry. I daresay she's a nice child. Only she does make you want to grab a fire-extinguisher. She burns with a hard gem-like flame."

"I very much wish that you had gone to St. Andrews, Richard, where you would have enjoyed the society of gentlemen, and not to that dreadful——"

"Ssh! I think she's coming down. And you mustn't be shocked."

"Shocked? If you don't shock me nothing will. What's wrong with her?"

"George is dressed like a boy scout. Or rather she protrudes from garments of that——"

"Be quiet."

There was a step on the staircase and George came in. Mrs. Cranston, before advancing, allowed herself a withering glance at her son. George was in a frock, miraculously uncreased. It was true that she remained more like Aurora than a mortal girl, and that the comparatively small areas of her person now exposed put to shame the toast which was presently carried into the room. But this was far from offending Cranston's mother—and it plainly delighted his father when he appeared. Indeed, it was presently plain to Cranston that George was going to be a great success. Mrs. Cranston gave her a rapid sketch of the families in the neighbourhood, with particular emphasis on the young men. Dr. Cranston enquired her age, height and weight and was accurately answered. George herself, without a glance at Cranston, remarked that she liked the simple Scottish ways. At home, Mum would let none of the boys sit down at table without a collar and tie.

Through all this only his real anxiety and a sense of the ticking clock preserved Cranston from merely childish gloom. The fact that the girl was a pure menace—and that she probably by now much disliked him as well—by no means made it any easier to drop his uncivil bombshell into the proceedings. But presently he did so, nevertheless. He had made unexpected arrangements on the previous night, he declared, and he was motoring south immediately after breakfast.

But the announcement fell flat. The fact came to him in what he knew to be a thoroughly foolish mingling of relief and resentment. If his mother thought his conduct outrageously rude, she dissimulated it in the distraction of calling for a fresh jar of marmalade. And presently she was sketching out picnics and tennis-parties designed, it seemed, to spread over a long vista of coming weeks. Gavin McGilvray would make an excellent partner for Georgiana; he was even taller than Richard and his backhand had become far better controlled. Dr. Cranston enquired about golf. It was clear that, as an entertainer, he saw no difficulty in stepping into his son's place. He had his busy times—he had been out on an emergency and had had to call a county ambulance that very morning—but then he had his easy times too. . . . Cranston was breathing freely, and had already bolted a second cup of coffee preparatory to rising and saying good-bye, when George abruptly succeeded in achieving what he had so notably failed at. She announced, amid general consternation, that as Richard was motoring south she would take the opportunity of travelling with him. This had been only a dash to Scotland, and she had heard of friends whom she must presently meet in London. But, if Mrs. Cranston allowed her, she would come back for a proper visit. And on this she was so specific, and prepared so unhesitatingly to name dates, that dismay was transformed into approval within five minutes. Mrs. Cranston saw great advantages in the proposal. Later in the summer, Richard would, of course, be at home to take her about, and numerous parties could be arranged well in advance.

Cranston listened in absolute dismay. The girl was outrageous. His sense of this—although in fact it rather lacked conviction—emboldened him to try something like blank refusal. "I'm frightfully sorry," he said, "but, you see——"

"You're not going alone? You haven't room?"

"Of course I'm going alone." He stopped. It was his first blank lie, and for a second he looked at her uncertainly. She was deplorable, without a doubt, but she didn't remotely mean any offence or aggression. The proposal had come into her head as absolutely licensed and, so to speak, graced by their vague cousinly relation— or perhaps just by some antipodean canon of normal human feeling. Nor, he realised, were his parents remotely within hail of thinking any evil of a plan which would send him off into the blue with a virtually unknown young woman. Their period sentiments were always shot with a large innocence. It was a fact of which he had become remorsefully if conveniently aware during the last few sultry weeks. He turned to George. "I meant that I'm afraid you wouldn't—you won't—be very comfortable in my terrible old car."

It was a remark which could only, in the circumstances, be received with mirth and jollity. George disappeared to get her rucksack and Mrs. Cranston to cut sandwiches. Cranston was left to the company of his father and the contemplation of an entirely new predicament to which he had committed himself. The real mischief, he saw, was the element of danger. Here at his mother's breakfast-table it had become hard to believe in. But it was there, all the same. A couple of miles away Sally was still doing duty with a gun, John Day was sitting helpless in that summer-house, and the man with the trilby hat lurked outside the castle—a figure of ruthless violence with incalculable forces already perhaps mustering behind him. All Cranston could now do was to set off with George and then in some way get rid of her. For instance, he could insult her. There were decidedly things for which he was sure that she wouldn't stand. He could——

Cranston's mind worked doubtfully forward in a series of displeasing images. He found that they were so displeasing as to be in fact impracticable. It struck him that he had better tell George the truth—or enough of it to convince her that he must go off on his own. But he could do this only after they had set out. To enter into the matter at all now was impossible.

His father was composedly reading *The Scotsman*. Something that he had recently let fall echoed oddly in Cranston's head. "Daddy," he asked, "what was that you said about an ambulance?"

"Yes—but too late. Dead, poor old soul." Dr. Cranston, absorbed in the London letter, answered concisely.

"It's gone back?"

Dr. Cranston glanced up briefly. "Not yet, I think. I arranged for the fellow to get some breakfast at the Dinwiddie Arms. An old friend of yours—before your expatriate period." Dr. Cranston was mildly caustic. "Be civil to this girl, by the way—even if she isn't a baronet's step-daughter and educated at Girton."

"Yes, of course." Cranston gave what he knew was a juvenile scowl.

"The Australian Cranstons have the high distinction, my dear boy, of sharing a great-grandfather with yourself. And he was a younger son of——"

"Bother the Australian Cranstons. . . . You don't mean Sandy Morrison?"

"Certainly I mean Sandy Morrison. He left his uncle a year ago and has been driving the ambulance for some time."

"I think I'll go across and look him up."

"To be sure." Dr. Cranston, because pleased, spoke as if in marked absence of mind. His feelings about great-grandfathers he found very easily reconcilable with others of a democratic cast, and both his sons had started at the village school. "Have you got enough money? I don't know what are the conventions when a young man gives a hitch to a hiking girl cousin." He chuckled. "But I imagine you might without offence offer to pay for a meal.

Not that the Australian Cranstons aren't extremely prosperous, I understand."

"Is that so?" Cranston in his turn was absent-minded. "I think I've got enough cash." He rose. "I'll just say good-bye to Elspeth."

"Say good-bye to Elspeth?" This time Dr. Cranston was genuinely astonished—indeed he eyed his son rather narrowly as he left the room. Then he returned to his newspaper. Curiosity however pricked him—he was after all a man of science—and presently he found himself going on tip-toe to the door. He was edified by a cautious whispering from a back passage.

"Master Richard—for shame! I'll do no such thing."

"Come on, Elspeth—there's no harm in it. Just for this once."

"No harm, indeed! It would be clean daft—and no' decent, foreby."

"If you don't, I'll tickle you till you scream—and leave you to explain to Mummy."

"It's outrageous, Master Richard. If you ask me, you just weren't enough skelpt as a bairn."

"I wasn't skelpt at all. Quick now—I'm in an awful hurry."

There was a sharp giggle—at the sound of which Dr. Cranston withdrew to his seat. When five minutes later his son returned to the room he looked at him somewhat doubtfully over the top of *The Scotsman*. "Really, Richard —have you been taking it into your head to woo your mother's mature Abigail for busses?"

"I don't know what you mean." Cranston grinned.

"Or, alternatively, you're a shocking old eavesdropper."

"And so I am. Your disease has a learned name, my boy."

"Rubbish."

"Gerontophilia, or sexual passion directed towards the aged. Think better of it, sir. There are maidens in Scotland more lovely by far, who would gladly be——"

"All right, Daddy—all right." Cranston heartily wished himself in a better position to relish this liberal paternal fooling. "But I wasn't, as a matter of fact. Kissing her, I mean." He hesitated. "I was borrowing something."

Dr. Cranston was alarmed. "Not a ten-shilling note? You used not to be above it. But you've just said——"

"No—not that. Something else. Will you promise me something?"

"Perhaps."

"Don't make a joke of it with Elspeth. Don't ask her when I'm gone."

For the first time, Dr. Cranston's brow clouded. There was something in this that lay outside the family conventions, and he was obscurely disturbed. "Richard," he asked, "is there anything in the wind? Have you been making a fool of yourself? Or are you up to something dangerous?"

"Both." Looking at his father, Cranston said this quite suddenly. "I have made a fool of myself. And I am up to something that's possibly dangerous—by way of getting clear."

"By way of getting clear of—a mess?" Dr. Cranston put *The Scotsman* down on the tablecloth. "You don't mean you're bolting from the consequences of some idiocy?"

"No. But I'm perhaps doing something a bit queer. It's by way of getting square with myself." He felt himself blush furiously. "A kind of debt of honour."

"And that's why you were so awkward about this girl? Shall I head her off—insist that she stop a bit?"

"No. I've got that fixed."

"I think I hear her coming downstairs with your

mother now." Dr. Cranston reached again for his paper. He was contriving a gallant appearance, his son saw, of having found their conversation satisfactory. "And I shall hold no converse with the outraged Abigail, my boy."

"Thank you."

"Drop me a line—if you feel prompted to, that is."

"Yes, Daddy."

"You can send it to the Infirmary, you know, if it's something with which you don't want to worry your mother."

"Yes—I see."

Dr. Cranston had risen and walked to the window. "Nice day for the run," he said. "Even in an awful car like yours."

CHAPTER IX

CRANSTON PULLED up in the village. The ambulance was still outside the Dinwiddie Arms. "I want to have a word with a schoolfellow," he explained. "Do you mind waiting?"

Without raising her eyes from the map she was studying, George shook her head. She was still in her frock—a deep yellow frock, so that she had the appearance of a portentously enormous sunflower. "I'll be seeing you," she said.

"He drives that ambulance."

"I see." For a second she took it as unremarkable. Then she looked surprised. "Didn't you go to Eton or somewhere?"

"I went there." He pointed across the village street.

"Where it says 'Infants'?" George was impressed.

He nodded. "Yes—and so did Sandy Morrison. I'm going to introduce him to you. We're all three going to do something together." He glanced cautiously at George. "At least I hope so."

"You didn't say anything about this at home."

"No more I did, George." He used her name for the first time. "But when I said I was going south alone I was fibbing."

She was disconcerted. "But, Richard, I asked if I was butting in."

"You're not. You're going to help. You see the castle on the map? I'm going to smuggle somebody out of it, and make hell-for-leather for London."

"Do you mean that I'm going to help at an elopement?"

George spoke coldly—and the effect struck him as so ludicrous that he had to smile. "I thought the Gretna Green business happened the other way on."

"It's a man, George—not a girl." He paused. "It's John Day."

"The scientist who disappeared? And he's now in Dinwiddie Castle?"

Cranston's estimate of the possible usefulness of George shot up. And that was how he had come to regard her. She was a great Amazonian creature who had blundered in, and she must take her chance. He would shove her out of the affair if real peril threatened. Short of that, she was expendable. After all, he hadn't scrupled to involve Sally—whom he had already wronged in ways that Sally might or might not know. So why not exploit this monster of a cousin? But he had been taking it for granted that the monster was shock-headed. Now he knew that he was wrong. Her way of taking the thing was in some indefinable way indicative of intelligence. "Yes," he said. "The scientist. He walked out of the sea and into my arms in the small hours of this morning."

"You mean that you were waiting for him? Is this Cold War stuff—with you active in it . . . on one side or another?"

"It was pure chance. And the Cold War aspect of John Day is over. He's a dying man. And he wants to see his wife."

"You're making it your business that he should?"

"Just that. He happens to be temporarily blinded, which makes things difficult. Will you help?"

"No." She looked at him seriously. "Not unless you convince me that you have to."

"I don't know if I can do that." Cranston paused—and as he did so it came to him like a revelation that he could tell this Amazonian intruder the whole thing. Or almost the whole thing. It might be brutal. He had the sense to know that a girl may not be the less maidenly for calling herself George and striding about the countryside in inconsiderable pants. He had not the slightest disposition to believe that Britomart herself had been more virginal. So if he told her she might hate it. But at least there was nothing between them that could be damaged by revelation. "Listen," he said. "It's simple, really. Day feels he acted unforgivably towards his wife, and that he has some sort of gesture—and no more than a gesture—to offer her. Well, he tumbled into my arms last night only because I was out fooling with a married woman. And it wasn't just fooling. There is something—I needn't go into it—that makes it vile. Mine's another unforgivable thing. And *my* gesture is to risk something, seeing this chap through."

George had gone very still, and for a moment he thought she was going to say nothing at all. And when she did speak it was with painful constraint. "I can't say I didn't ask for it—your story. Which doesn't mean that you should have told it, all the same."

"I'm sorry."

"Or am I being a fool? Probably I am. . . . And what do you mean by risking something?"

"Being killed, for one thing. There was shooting last night. The chaps to whom he's given the slip are out for his blood—and that of anybody holding in with him."

"Very understandably, I'd say."

"Yes. But there's another risk, less easy to express. If Day had murdered somebody, or was a wicked blackmailer, or a defaulting financier or something of that sort, I'd only be risking—and inviting you to risk—being uncomfortably packed off to gaol. But behind Day—and willynilly all around him still—the issues are tremendous.

He may have vitally important information which some
Cabinet Minister, or old colleague, or efficient policeman
could show him he ought to come out with. I may keep
him away from these people only to see him successfully
hunted down and killed by his former employers. And
there are other possibilities. I'm risking—well, having to
admit that I've been an irresponsible ass in rather a big
way."

"It's an awkward situation, Richard—I agree."

"It's a regular cow, George."

She faintly smiled. "We'd better get on. What do I
do?"

"Could you impersonate a Scottish housemaid?"

"Better, I suppose, than I could impersonate a Scottish
countess. But I couldn't manage the accent."

"That won't matter. You'll only be talking to a
foreigner—and then no more than a few words."

"Don't housemaids in this part of the world dress in a
particular way?"

"I've got the proper clothes in the back. I borrowed
them from our maid at home. Only I'm afraid they'll be
on the small side."

"But I'm used to giving rather skimpy effects?" George
was amused at the discomfort this thrust occasioned him.
"Do I have to do things with your Sandy Morrison?"

Cranston shook his head, and climbed out of the car.
"No. But if I can't nail him to do his own turn we'll have
to think again. Sit tight. I'm going in to try."

"Hullo, Sandy."

"Good morning, Mr. Cranston."

This was unpromising, and Cranston took cautious
stock of his erstwhile fellow scholar. With one hand Sandy
was frugally rotating a crust in the last of the bacon fat

on his plate, while with the other he drained a large mug of tea. They had dressed him decorously in some approximation to uniform for the purpose of driving the ambulance—but he was discernably Sandy Morrison still. He was freckled and snub-nosed and tousle-haired, with a dour pious expression and a glint of dangerous mischief in his eye. Cranston contrived to look at him insolently. "Is that the way they've taught you to talk, you silly loon?"

Sandy set down his mug. "It isn't often that we have the pleasure of seeing you in the north, sir."

Cranston advanced and towered above him. "I could take you by the lug," he said, "and haul you behind the kirk, and hammer you till you were roaring like a two-headed calf, Sandy Morrison. And that would learn you good morning and pleasure of seeing you in the north."

Sandy got to his feet. "And could you that?"

"That I could—as I did the first day that ever I had sight of your ill features—Sandy Snotnose."

"Then come awa'—Dickie-Big-Doup." Sandy was breathing wrathfully.

Cranston sat down. "Sandy," he whispered, "are you for a splore?"

"The devil take you, Dick." Sandy sat down too. His expression was now less pious than sanctimonious, but the glint in his eye was correspondingly wilder. "Can't you see, man, that they've turned me respectable? The ambulance is probation. If I pass I'm to have the hearse." He paused and dropped his voice. "Is it salmon?"

"Nothing of the kind. It's just to drive your ambulance up to the castle and through the gates. And to bide there a while not much noticing things. And then to come away again."

Sandy looked apprehensive. "Is it something to dae wi' a quean?"

108

"It is not. I'm not one that goes after women."

"It's no' to dae wi' her leddyship there?"

"No." Cranston had a moment of panic. His madness —his late madness—must have become gossip already. "I want to smuggle a man out of the place, Sandy—and without some that may be watching knowing it."

"I'm to be back at the Infirmary in the forenoon."

"And so you shall be." Cranston rose. "I've got my car—and somebody in it who's helping me. I'll drive to the head of the glen and park in the quarry. Do you follow in five minutes, Sandy. After that, the whole thing won't take half an hour."

"It's clean skite, Dick Cranston, and I canna thole such daftness." Sandy rose resignedly. "When I drive in, what am I to tell the creature Patullo at the lodge?"

"You're to tell him it's an emergency, and then drive on past the first turn in the drive. Then you stop, and I get out and fetch the man I'm speaking of. He's in the old garden now. And then we drive away and go back to the quarry."

"And Patullo when he lets me out again?"

"You're to say it was all a mistake, and that it's not Dinwiddie you should be at, but Dindervie."

"And what o' Sir Alex? Suppose he's up and ploutering, and syne finds an ambulance in his drive. Won't he be dumbfoundered?"

"You must scratch your head, Sandy, like a regular daftie, and have nothing sensible to say of yourself. He'll do no more than turn you out, and make a great joke of your gormless wandering. . . . But now listen. Later to-day, or perhaps to-morrow or the next day, strangers may come checking up on you, asking what took the ambulance to Dinwiddie. You'll say it was an emergency call for the cook there, and that the poor soul is now in the

Infirmary having her appendix out. You're to say that, and nothing more or other, to any stranger or foreign creature that asks. Because somebody else is going to be telling the same story."

"It seems there's a muckle o' falsehood being required o' me for auld acquaintance sake, Dick Cranston." And Sandy shook his head gloomily. "We maun hope your foreign creatures don't do their speiring on the Sabbath."

Sally's vigil had lasted rather longer than he had intended. But at least he had turned the general awkwardness of the morning to positive account. Or he would have done so if this plan worked. To get Day away from the castle unobserved so that the man with the tribly hat would still be left guessing, would be an unexpected gain. And now the success or failure of his stratagem was imminent. The ambulance had swung out of the glen and the castle was straight ahead. Cranston glanced across at George. "You understand your instructions?"

She nodded—and then frowned at what must have been an incautious grin. "I'm a tremendous figure of fun?" she asked.

He allowed the grin cheerfully to grow. "Do you remember whether Phoebus Apollo had a sister?"

"No—I don't."

"A *big* sister? Well, if she existed, and was banished from Calydon to Caledonia, and took service in a manse, succeeding to attire which the minister's wife had judged suitable and adequate for some merely mortal handmaiden——"

"Shut up!" He believed she was really angry. "I don't mind the cap, or even this idiotic starched apron. But these black woollen stockings I pretty well can't stand."

"They scratch? You must just thole them, as Sandy

there would say, for ten minutes more." Cranston peered out. "And now, George, get ready. We'll be stopping between the gate-houses while old Patullo opens up. That means that for a minute we'll be quite cut off from any possibility of close observation. So when you nip out and stroll down the road, you'll appear to have come out from the castle. You've got the letter?"

"Here."

"The pillar-box is at the foot of the hill. The castle folk don't really use it, but the chap won't know that—just as he won't know that Melbourne and not that manse framed your accents."

"You think he'll really come?"

"It's a pretty good bet. . . . Watch the gates as you walk back, and try not to reach them until they're opening again. Ten to one the chap will have strolled away a bit after pumping you, and you'll be able to slip back in here quite undetected. If Patullo sees, he may think it a bit queer, but he's a stupid old boy and will have a dim notion you're a nurse."

"We're slowing down. Is this it?"

"Yes." Cranston put a hand on the door of the ambulance and pushed it open. "*Now!*" he said.

She was gone. He closed the door. There was a murmur of voices—Sandy blathering and Patullo havering, he thought—and then the ambulance moved forward again. Presently it turned a corner and stopped. He thrust the door wide open and jumped out. Sandy was looking round at him apprehensively. "Dick," he said, "what if that dreich auld Patullo telephones up tae the castle and doon comes the laird? They'll never gie me the hearse if——"

"Turn round, Sandy. And dinna fash. I'll be back with my man in five minutes."

Cranston turned and ran. The old inner ward was the awkward stretch, because parts of the modern building commanded it. After that he had the cover of the ruined shell-keep until he had gained the garden. What would he do if he bumped into Sir Alex—or even into Caryl, limping about with her martyred ankle? But he was all right for the moment—safe in the garden and making full tilt for the summer-house. He glimpsed Sally—she was sitting precisely where he had left her—and saw her wave. "Day," he called, "are you ready? We'll be away in no time."

"I'm glad to hear it. I've been wondering." Day's voice was conversational and unreproachful. "I still see damned little. But I'd no longer run straight into a tree."

"Then, come along. But better take my hand to make sure. I've arranged a private departure for the south."

"Splendid."

The return through the garden was less rapid, but without disaster. Sandy had turned the ambulance and Cranston thrust Day into it. "Right!" he called. "But don't forget the girl."

"The girl?" Day was instantly questioning. "The step-daughter?"

"No, no—not Sally. Somebody else I've had to bring in to help. I'll tell you later. Keep quiet." The ambulance had stopped. He could hear Patullo grumbling. He was a surly old brute. But this held one advantage: to any stranger's questioning he would be unlikely to offer any response at all.

They were through the gates. He could hear Patullo banging them to. The ambulance was crawling. He opened the door. George tumbled in. "Can I take them off?" she asked.

Cranston laughed aloud. "Elspeth's stockings?" He

felt an extraordinary exhilaration in the sense that Dinwiddie was behind them. "This minute, if you like. And the whole outfit, as soon as we get back to the quarry." He took a deep breath. "May I introduce John Day? Day, this is my cousin Georgiana Cranston from Australia." He turned to her. "Did it happen?"

"The encounter? You're telling me. But it wasn't a Slavonic gentleman with a trilby hat. It was an American lady with field-glasses and a camera."

"Oh!" Cranston was disconcerted. "Perhaps there was nothing in it. Perhaps it was just chance."

"I don't think so." George had sat down on a species of stretcher and was composedly rolling off the offending stockings. "In a casual way, she was much too much on the spot. Was this romantic pile Dinwiddie Castle—and did I work there? There wasn't much in that. But she wanted to know about the ambulance. So I told her your story about our poor cook. I said that the letter I was posting was to poor cook's married daughter in Glasgow telling her that her mother had been taken poorly. Was taken poorly right?"

"Not bad."

"I didn't forget to call her madam. And then she asked if we had a lot of visitors, and if any had just arrived. So I said no, I was sure nobody had. And then I turned shy and came away."

George, who had delivered all this with some complacency, glanced at her now bare feet and then tucked them away beneath the stretcher. Cranston turned to Day. "What do you think?"

"That they could muster one or two agents pretty quickly . . . and any number quite soon. My guess is that it wasn't just an idle tourist."

"I'm sure it wasn't." George, although she was studying

Day with attention, spoke crisply. "I left her and walked back up the road. But just before I turned into the gate-house I took a look round. She had climbed a bank and was scanning a high stone wall—is it the garden wall?—towards the cliff. And then she put up a hand and waved. It wasn't—well, one tourist's wave to another who has gone astray. In fact, it wasn't a wave at all. It was a signal."

There was a moment's silence in the swaying ambulance. Sandy Morrison was driving fast. George, Cranston thought, had no particular flair for the dramatic. Nevertheless, her last words had touched an ominous note. And it was Day who spoke. "Could you say what sort of signal?"

"It was a slow horizontal movement with one arm. I'd say she was giving a negative report."

"And so far, so good." Cranston nodded confidently. "They're left quite at sea about what has happened in the last seven or eight hours. All the same, we mustn't waste time. It looks as if, even in that quarry, we mightn't escape observation for long. . . . And here we are." The ambulance had stopped. Cranston braced himself. "Listen, George. You've been wonderful. And now Day and I will hop out, and you can change into your own things."

"No, you don't."

He was confused. "What do you mean?"

"You don't bundle Mr. Day into your car and make off quietly while I'm turning into your exasperating cousin again. If you don't promise me to wait, I come as I am."

"George, you've been involved quite enough in this. Probably we're now going to show those people a clean pair of heels. But we can't be sure. And it just isn't right that you should be——"

"But you've got to get me out of this, Richard. Think of that woman. She'd recognise me again in a flash—ghastly stockings or no ghastly stockings. And where should I be, supposing she and her friends came upon me defence-lessly tramping through these wilds? I've earned your protection Richard Cranston, and I claim it."

George, it seemed, could manage drama after all. In a way, she was just being too clever for him. At the same time, there was a positive truth in the proposition with which she had trapped him. He ought to have thought of it. It was a sober fact that he had involved this girl not only in an episode of danger but in a continuing danger—whether they parted or kept together.

"All right," he said. "I promise."

"Then out you get, both of you. And I think I'll get into my walking things again, rather than that frock. If you don't mind, that is to say."

"I don't care tuppence." Aware that this was rather a boorish reply, Cranston made the more haste to throw open the door of the ambulance. The action revealed Sandy Morrison, scratching his tousled head and gazing round the deserted quarry in slow consternation. "Sandy," he called out, "what's taken you?"

"It's no' onything that's tak'n me, ye great gaup. It's some loon that's tak'n your auld rattletrap."

Cranston leapt to the ground. A single glance told him that Sandy spoke the truth. His car was gone.

CHAPTER X

"Y ou're sure it's the same place?" Day spoke from the interior of the ambulance. He had not been prevented by Sandy Morrison's inelegant vocabulary from tumbling instantly to what had happened.

"Of course it's the same place—damn you!" Hearing himself swear, Cranston knew that he was rattled. His plan had been clever—but it looked as if somebody else had been cleverer still. And there was this girl. She was a tiresome irruption, certainly, from her uncouth wilderness. But she had played up very decently. And now he had allowed himself to land her in a trap. A single quick look round this lonely quarry had left him with no illusions. It was not the sort of spot in which professional car-thieves find it profitable to lurk. His car had vanished as a move—probably a final and decisive move—in the melo-drama in which this accursed John Day had involved him.

"In that case we know where we are." Day's tone had all its irritating calm.

"And what the hell does it matter to you?" Cranston rounded on him stupidly. "You're going to die—aren't you? But we don't all share your blasted simple plan. Do you think I want to see this girl riddled with bullets—or Sandy here, or myself?"

"I'm sure you don't. And that being so, perhaps we should attempt to drive on in this ambulance. It's what they call a forlorn hope."

"We can try." Recovering himself, Cranston swung round quickly. "Sandy, climb in—and drive for all you're worth. I'll explain later. But it's life or death, I promise you."

"But, man, I've got to be back in the forenoon!" Sandy raised a protesting wail. "Gin I jine in your daft ploy ony mair, d'ye think I'll ever hae that hearse?"

"You'll have a hearse, all right—if we don't get out of this." It was Day who spoke, and again impassively. "But first, they'll have to collect what's left of you with a shovel."

"And what sort of a daft speak is that, ye plook-faced——"

A sharp report from the edge of the quarry made Sandy break off. It was followed by a quick hiss of escaping air. Cranston turned round in time to see one of the rear wheels settle flat on its rim. By a single neat shot the ambulance had been virtually immobilised.

So that was that. Cranston took a quick survey of the terrain and acknowledged—what he already knew—that it could not be worse. Behind them, in an unbroken semicircle, was the face of the quarry. In front was the unfrequented road leading to the glen and to the moors beyond. On the other side of the road a bare brae rose gently to a sky-line perhaps a couple of hundred yards away. The enemy was presumably looking down from somewhere at the top of the quarry. Even if no more than a single person lurked there, it was a position admirably chosen. There was no conceivable line of flight that offered the slightest hope of a successful get-away. . . . He found that George was standing beside him. "Get back," he said. "Get back at once."

"Nonsense. I was brought up on this." Very deliberately, she took a dozen paces into the open. And he saw suddenly that she was an extraordinary sight. His joke about Apollo's big sister had been only too near the mark; she was a divinity disguised as divinities must be disguised in opera—with grotesque inadequacy. In Elspeth's clothes she had the appearance of some resplendent symbol of earth—say a great sheaf of corn—unconvincingly masquerading as a scare-crow. That whole business at the castle had been too clever by half. Or rather it had been too light-hearted—the sort of thing one contrives in a rag, and not in a desperate battle for survival. He watched her with compunction as she strolled back to him.

"I mean, of course, in my reading. Bush-rangers. Here's a coach or a waggon, and there"—she pointed upwards to the lip of the quarry—"is Ned Kelly. . . . Sandy Morrison, did you ever hear of Ned Kelly?"

Cranston realised that the incredible girl was acting with deliberation and in the interest of Sandy's morale. Something of the sort was needed, for this was plainly his baptism of fire and he had been a little taken aback by it. Now he grinned slowly, although his eye was apprehensively on the quarry. "I've seen something like," he said, "at the picture-hoose in Dindervie. Ye mind the way they end episodes in the serials? A fine skirry-whirry we're landit in."

"Will they do . . . absolutely anything?" She had turned to Cranston. "Is this it?"

He nodded. "Yes," he said quietly. "I'm terribly sorry—and it seems incredible. But they're—well, entirely serious."

"Then I propose to get into other clothes." George swung herself back into the ambulance. "And you needn't turn out our purblind friend. I don't mind him. But I do mind going to my last account dressed like something in Sir James Barrie."

"Day—come out!" Cranston had realised what he must do. "We're beaten."

"So soon?" Day came to the rear of the ambulance but made no move to emerge. George was wasting no time; Cranston could see her scrambling out of her dress in the semi-darkness beyond. "Right at the start, in fact?" Day was almost mocking. "Is that what you call resource?"

"Don't be a fool, man. They've caught us, and the circumstances leave only one thing to do. Will you do it?"

"I think I know what you mean." Day paused and appeared to be listening carefully. "Doesn't it strike you as odd that they seem in no hurry with their next move? My guess is that it's just as it was last night. There's only one man. He's taken your car, and he's got us, I suppose, neatly immobilised. There's no cover to get away behind?"

"Not a scrap."

"On the other hand, he may be immobilised too."

Cranston shook his head. "I don't see it. Again, it's just like last night. All he need do is come over and blow our brains out."

"He can't be certain that by this time we haven't got a gun—or several guns—ourselves." Day was patiently expository, like a teacher before a dull class. "He may be reckoning that he can do no more than just pin us here until some of his associates turn up. Actually, something else may turn up instead—and entirely to our advantage. It's unlikely, but one never knows. So I don't at all see that we need throw up the sponge. Courage, my dear young man, courage."

"My guess is that they've mustered quite a force by now." Cranston kept his temper with difficulty. "And if they simply open up on us here there'll be a massacre—

including this girl. I think you'd better consider whether it isn't up to you——"

"To go quietly?" Day asked the question reasonably. "To walk straight towards the cliff or quarry or whatever it is and let them finish me? You think they'd then let the rest of the party off?"

"I want you to come with me—you need a guiding hand, after all—and talk to them, whoever they are."

"You're a fool. You don't know them." Day was sharply impatient. "They'd shoot us down, I tell you, and then turn on the others. They're going to leave no witness of this. Our only——"

"*Mr. John Day!*"

Cranston swung round. The voice had come from somewhere high up in the quarry—and even as he searched the rock the figure of a man stood boldly up on the sky-line and then dropped out of sight again.

"*Mr. John Day!*" It was a second voice—and simultaneously a second figure rose momentarily into view. The first had been English; this was markedly foreign.

"*Mr. John Day—please!*" A third voice, also foreign, quickly followed, and again the owner briefly showed himself. But this time the same voice continued to speak from cover. "Will Mr. John Day please join us? Nobody else need come. Will Mr. John Day kindly join us?"

The summons was utterly bizarre—like the call of a pageboy in a nightmarish hotel. But Day appeared unperturbed by it. "You see? They're not really anxious to present themselves in person. But they'd be quite willing to get on with the job from a distance. I'd advise the young man and yourself to come inside."

Cranston thought for a moment. "Sandy—can we make a dash for it? We can drive on as we are?"

"Aye, Dick—we can that, at a kin o' crawl. But ye

120

maun mind they've got your rattletrap—and mebbe a car o' their ain foreby roon the next bend. It's an unco awkward thing." Sandy scratched his head again. "I dinna ken what for's a' this stour. Thae voices are fair scunnererfu' and I canna' thole them. But I'm thinking I hear an engine. Might it be the polis, do you think, in their bit car from Dindervie?"

Cranston listened. There was certainly an odd throb or rumble in the air. But it didn't sound like a car. "Farm machinery somewhere," he said. . . . "Listen."

Again one of the voices was speaking from the quarry. This time it was nearer, and from lower down on the left. "We're coming," it said. "I think you have a lady? There need be no violence—nothing distressing. Simply an appointment with Mr. Day. We advise him to join us."

"Awa' and bile your heids!" Suddenly moved to wrath, Sandy Morrison made the quarry ring with this rude injunction. Then he made a dash for the cabin of his ambulance, and reappeared brandishing a spanner. "I'll learn ye!" he bawled. "Come awa' doon here, ye lurking loupers, and I'll learn ye."

It was a challenge that was immediately accepted. There was a whistle from somewhere in the quarry, and two men appeared simultaneously at each end of it. A fifth rose up from behind a heap of stone straight in front of them. Cranston caught a glint on his face that he recognised. He had doffed his trilby, but there could be no doubt about his identity. All the men began to advance with deliberation in a contracting half-circle. They were all much like the man in the middle. They all wore the same sort of townee clothes. If anything could be more sinister than the simple fact of their threatening advance it was this displeasing incongruity with their surroundings.

They should have been lurking under lamp-posts in disreputable streets or keeping furtive observation on others of their own kind in undesirable pubs.

The advance continued. The men made no display of weapons, but each kept one hand in a pocket of his jacket. George dropped to the ground again beside Cranston. She was once more in her khaki walking kit. "It's not quite real—is it?" Her voice was steady. "It ought to be flickering faintly—and in glorious Technicolor." She was watching the man with the glinting glasses. "And they ought to keep on coming at us until they're enormously larger than life."

"Life-size will do." From behind them in the ambulance Day's voice for the first time was savage. "There's no sign of traffic in this damned solitude you've trapped us in? Don't I hear something?"

Even as Day spoke the line of men came to a halt. The throb and rumble in the air had rapidly increased— and now there was added to it a sort of clattering tramp, as of an army of booted giants pounding up the road to the glen. Cranston swung round. What was in fact advancing upon them was a line of tanks.

The uproar grew. A second line of the monsters had appeared over the brae straight ahead. They had enormous guns that gave them the appearance of a herd of trumpeting elephants. And they came lumbering and lurching down the hill, apparently intent upon a rendezvous with their fellows at this point where the quarry made a great scar on the answering slope. For a second Cranston stared unbelievingly. He could think of the irruption only in terms of a planned spectacular act of rescue, and the forces being hurled into the battle seemed fantastically disproportioned to their task. Then he realised that the appearance was of course fortuitous. The tanks had no interest in the ambulance standing in the quarry. And presently they would be gone.

He turned round again. The five men had vanished. Very understandably, this abrupt appearance of the armed forces of the Crown had a little thrown them out of their stride.

"It's thae Tank Corps chiels frae the camps ahint Drumtoul. They've been scurryvaiging ouer the moors these ten days syne. It's tairrible bad for the birrds." Sandy was wholly disapproving. "And they'll no' even gae lounlie on the sabbath. The meenister at Auchinputtock has preached a sairmon on it."

When not more than twenty yards away, the first of the monsters drew to a halt. One by one, lurching, coughing and spluttering, the others did the same. There was a long line of them on the road. Those on the brae had spread out as they descended, and they were now immobile on its slopes as if they had been frozen while they grazed. Trapdoors opened and beret-clad heads looked out. A group of officers appeared from nowhere and applied themselves to conversing importantly over a map. Some of the beret clad heads, becoming aware of George, emitted significant whistles and cautiously improper cries. Cranston glanced at the girl. "Well," he said, "Day was right. Something *has* turned up. And I'd better go and nobble that Major."

"No!" She put an urgent hand on his arm. "You wouldn't think of throwing up the sponge if you didn't feel you had me on your hands. Sandy and you must change the wheel, and get clean away from under their noses. If you like, I'll stop behind."

"With the licentious soldiery?"

"I expect they'll be frightfully decent. The Major looks most fatherly."

"Sandy, man—come on." Cranston made a dive for the tool-kit. "We'll get away yet."

"And that we will." Sandy Morrison dropped the spanner with which he had armed himself and went to work furiously. The ambulance was jacked up before he spoke again. "Dick," he said in a low voice, "ye'll no really leave the quean-bairn wi' the sodjers?"

"We ought to, Sandy. You see now what sort of a business this is. It's not for a girl."

"I dinna' ken that she's ony less apt to it than ye are yersel', Dickie Cranston. See her getting oot the spare whiles you dae na' mair than stand by like a gumphie." Sandy was withering. Then he paused to draw from a pocket an enormous watch. "I can get ye a' to Drumtoul halt, man, in time for the wee diesel-car tae the junction. And there ye can tak' the express. Hae ye siller?"

"Quite a lot. And Day claims to have a fortune."

"Does he that?" Sandy spoke with respect. "Haud the thing fast, man, whiles I get the nuts off. The tanks are no' for moving yet?"

"No, thank goodness. Some of the men are out on the heather and smoking. My guess is that the Major has got lost and won't admit it."

"Praise the Lord!" Sandy ejaculated this with genuine piety. "And the preen-heidit foo's in the quarry?"

"They're not so witless, if you ask me. But they're giving no sign."

"We'll jink them yet. . . . Right, lassie—pass it ou'er." Sandy took the spare-wheel from George with an approving nod. "Ye're warth twa o' this feckless loon Dickie. Ye'll hae the hearse, mebbe, afore mysel'. There's a lum-hat gaes wi' it. You'd look braw in that." Sandy laughed extravagantly at this fantasy. "Praise-be-thankit, it's on." Sandy looked up, and paused indignantly. Several of the more enterprising youths from the tank-crews had slipped across the road and formed an admiring group round the ambulance. Ostensibly they were appraising the technique of its driver. But their real interest was, of course, in George. The classically educated among them might have likened her to an Amazon, dropped in, appropriately girt, to do a turn of work in Vulcan's smithy. The bolder could be heard comparing her points, audibly and favourably, with those of such young ladies as had recently figured on the front page of *Blighty*. Sandy tightened a final nut with energy. "It's no daecent," he said. "A loon has but tae put on a bit uniform and syne he sheds a' the godliness that was skelpit into him as a wean. Awa' wi' ye!" He looked up and waved an oily hand at the young men. "First scaring the birrds that ought to be reservit for the gentry in the lodges and the half-gentry in the hotels. And then making profane talk aboot the fore and aft o' a maiden that's worth the pack o' ye. Awa', I say."

Much as if endorsing the injunction, the Major at this point gave a shout, and somebody farther back blew a whistle. The soldiers went off at the double. Tanks here and there began to snort and shake themselves. George finished strapping the punctured wheel into its place and turned to Sandy. "Where will they be going?"

"Back to Drumtoul for their brose. Eating by day, and sprunting after the village lasses by nicht, is a' they're fit for."

"Then we can go too." George gave a single glance at Cranston—too swift to be an appeal—and swung herself up into the seat beside the driver's. In a moment Sandy had followed her.

Cranston picked up the jack and pitched it into the ambulance. He took a careful look at the quarry. There was no sign of the enemy, but he had no doubt that they were still lurking there. The first of the tanks were already moving. It was clear that the exercise was in fact over, and that they were minded to trundle decorously home. He glanced into the ambulance. Day was sitting quietly on a stretcher. In Sir Alex Blair's expensive tweeds and the dark glasses he was unrecognisable. Cranston could almost persuade himself that here was somebody with whom he had nothing to do. But that, unfortunately, would be an illusion. "You were right," he said abruptly. "And we're getting away. For the moment."

"It's from moment to moment, my dear fellow, that I've lately learned to live." Day stretched himself. "We've picked up some sort of miraculous convoy to a place called Drumtoul?"

"Just that. As my friend here would say, the deil looks after his ain."

"How long until we get there?"

"At the pace we're likely to make with this circus, I'd say over an hour."

"Then I think—do you know?—I'll sleep. There's nothing like swimming for making you drowsy." Day yawned, and then placidly lay down.

For a second Cranston stared at him. Day, he was sure, was not posing. Lying there, he was perfectly relaxed. Relaxation was for the moment the rational thing, and the man was able to command it. He himself, on the other hand, felt his heart thumping and his limbs trembling. He was no longer frightened of being afraid, but he couldn't remotely pretend that he wasn't in a state of tension. "In that case," he said shortly, "I'll get in with them in front."

Day made no reply. He was taking off the dark glasses and settling himself on the stretcher. The ambulance had a faint antiseptic smell that made Cranston think of his father's surgery. George's rucksack and Elspeth's abandoned clothes were lying in one corner. For some reason he had a sudden sharp vision of Sally—of Sally at a summer dance, very exquisite and rather beautiful. . . . He shut the door with a snap, ran round to the front of the ambulance and scrambled up. "There's room?" he asked.

George nodded without speaking. She was watching the line of tanks. "There!" she said suddenly to Sandy. He slipped into gear and the ambulance jolted over the floor of the quarry and inserted itself neatly between one tank and another. "Will they mind, do you think?"

"They'll only mind that they're shut down in their daft contraiptions and no' able to be casting their immodest regard upon your person." Sandy gave her a sidelong glance that was entirely austere. "And they canna' bid us pass and go ahead, sin frae here through tae Drumtoul the road's scarce wide enough for the muckle-douped things theirsel's."

"Is it a long climb?"

"Aye—we climb right tae the top o' the moor. You and Mr. Cranston here will be able to look awa' doon tae the sea and tak' a last glink at Dinwiddie Castle. If it's ony satisfaction tae either of you."

CHAPTER XI

For some time they were silent as the long line of monsters laboured towards the summit of the moor. They were out of the glen and the heather rolled away monotonously on either side of them, unrelieved except by a line of shooting-butts a mile on their left and here and there a deserted sheep-fold piled up out of weathered grey stone. A burn ran by the side of the road, its murmur entirely drowned by the clatter before and behind them. It was hard not to believe that the whole moor was exhaling exhaust gases. Presently Cranston pointed ahead. "You see that cairn?" he said to George. "The road goes off on a long curve there. If we look back, we should be able to see the whole line behind us—and tell if they've joined in."

"Whether they have or not, I suppose they're unlikely just to give up? They really feel Day to be terrifically important?"

Cranston nodded. "I'm sure they do. There was a big effort—and a lightning effort—getting five chaps on top of us like that. What more they can mobilise, I've no idea. But everything they've got. Within twelve hours, I'd say, everything they've got in these islands."

"Sandy—do you hear that?" George appeared to be in remarkably good spirits. "You are at grips with the entire forces of atheistic communism."

"Maybe I am, Miss. But I maun be back at the Infirmary the forenoon, all the same. I canna' see the Superintendent, coarse chiel that he is, making much o' a tale o' Sandy Morrison at grips wi' the Kremlin. . . . If you want to spy back adoon the road, there's a pair o' glasses in the bag at your fut."

Cranston stooped and rummaged. Presently he produced a pair of excellent binoculars. "And what, Sandy," he asked, "is the use you find for these?"

"Bird watching." Sandy was dour. "It's an improving ploy, Dick Cranston, that you must mind them urging us to in the school." He gave a swift wicked grin. "I'm a great one for keeping an eye on the birds."

"You're a great one for keeping an eye on Lord Urquhart's or Sir Alex's keepers, if you ask me." Cranston leant far out of the window and scanned the curve of road behind them. "There's nothing. Only tanks, and more tanks. If they're after us, it's not at the tail-end of this queer procession. . . . George, have you got your maps?"

"They're in the rucksack in the back—unless Day's eaten them. Why?"

"Just that it strikes me——" Cranston broke off. "There's the sea," he said. "And there's the castle."

"Dinwiddie?"

"Dinwiddie." For a moment he continued to stare. The place was bumping up and down in his field of vision, but he had it perfectly in focus. It seemed very near—and there was a queer shock in its suddenly being so. Part ruin and part mansion, it stood out boldly on its cliff against a sea still silvery in the morning light. And somehow it was ominous and evil. He tried to recall the sharp vision of Sally that he had experienced only half an hour before. But all he saw was Caryl's flesh in moonlight—that and her husband Alex Blair, spruce and polished and facetious. He handed the glasses silently to George, and sat back so that she could focus them across his chest. For some horrible seconds he was gripped by what he thought of as his dream-feeling—the sense of a sudden recollection, seizing the mind as it swam up out of oblivion, of an irrevocable thing done. . . . "Clear—isn't it?" He had forced himself to speak.

"There's something I don't like about it."

"Something *you* don't like?" He was vastly struck by this.

"I don't like mediæval things." George was puzzled, yet decided. "I thought I'd find them marvellous. But the Tower cured me."

"The Tower of London—you've been there?" He was amused.

"Of course I've been there. It's horrifying. Do you realise that London was once a Roman city—a civilised place that you and I would recognise? And that centuries and centuries later, all that people could manage was a ghastly mixture of slum and prison—like the Tower, or like Castle This and Castle That? It's terrifying. It shows how civilisation can just seep away."

"I suppose it does. But the mediæval people built the cathedrals. Have you seen them?"

"You can build cathedrals without knowing about drains—or even baths." George lowered the binoculars for a moment and looked at him with what appeared to be perfect seriousness. "And when did they put baths into Dinwiddie? Probably not more than fifty years ago."

Cranston laughed. Five minutes before, it was something he would have believed himself become permanently incapable of. "Do all Australians believe that godliness is next to cleanliness?"

"There's something coming out." George had the glasses focused once more on the castle. "It must be a tradesman's van. It's a brilliant yellow. But it's going very fast."

"Yellow?" Suddenly he remembered. "But that's

130

Blair's car—Sir Alex Blair's Cadillac." He laughed again. "Would you expect a Scottish baronet—and an intellectual one at that—to paint a Cadillac bright yellow?"

"I'm afraid I don't know at all."

"Well, you wouldn't. But there's something odd in him."

"Blair? What is he, anyway?"

"What I've just told you—a baronet, and our local bigwig Number Two. He comes after old Lord Urquhart, who's his deadly enemy. And he's a physicist—a *ci-devant* physicist, I should say. He was on the way to eminence when the baronetcy—and something soft inside him, I expect—stepped in and sank him."

"He might have been what John Day is?"

Cranston stared at her. "Well, yes—but there's something decidedly *ci-devant* about Day too now, I'd say."

"In rather a different sense." George had swept the binoculars round in a curve. "I suppose Cadillacs are pretty hot? It's travelling very fast indeed."

"It's a pleasure to hear o' something that's no behaving like a funeral." Sandy Morrison was peevish. "I'll no mind crawling like this when I'm set up wi' my hearse. 'Twill be but reverent-like. But an ambulance is anither matter. I've got a wee bit bell here—doon there at my fut—that's for clearing the traffic awa' frae in front o' me in the toon. D'ye think, Dick, I might gie a bit ding wi' it noo?"

"It wouldn't do the slightest good. The pace of this whole column is set by someone in an armoured car at the front."

"Yin o' the high heed-yins, nae doot." Sandy was disgusted. "The great dunderclunk might hae a thought tae my Superintendent." He pulled out his watch again.

"Frae Drumtoul tae the Infirmary's nae sma' loup. And I mun mak' it in the forenoon."

"We're not likely to forget it." Cranston turned to George. "What would you say they know about us?"

"That here we are. And perhaps that's about enough. I suppose there are other roads to this Drumtoul."

"There certainly are. But what would they know about us once we definitely broke the trail?"

"One of them has seen me close-up—in that queer rig. Five of them have seen the two of us—and Sandy—at a middle distance. As for Day, I suppose at least one of them knows him very well. But do they know about his eyes?"

Cranston shook his head. "I don't see that they can. At least, it would be something worth taking a risk on. But what isn't worth taking a risk on is driving into Drumtoul in this ambulance. And that's why I asked you about your maps. . . . Sandy, would you have the nerve to stop?"

"And what for no?" Sandy was indignant. "Hae I no a right to halt upon the guid Queen's highway for my lawful occasions—whether or no' all the Queen's tanks are a wee bit impeded the while?" Sandy paused. "Are ye thinking, man, o' taking to the heather?"

"Yes, I am."

"Wi' Miss Cranston here and the blinter?"

"Day's eyes are the trouble, all right—and have been from the start. But I've got a plan."

"Ye aye had plans as a wean, Dickie Cranston, and fair daft some o' them were."

"That's true enough. My plan at the castle this morning was daft. But I think I've thought of a better one."

"Which is?"

"I'm not going to tell you."

"Ye'll no' let on tae your auld schoolfellow?" Sandy was deeply offended. "And would it be owerweening, Mr. Cranston, to spier what for no'?"

"If you don't know you can't tell. Not even if the Kremlin catches you in a corner and asks you not too gently."

"Lordsake!" Not unnaturally, Sandy received this with some dismay. "Are you telling me they'd accord me waur than death?"

Cranston nodded. "Undoubtedly. But fortunately their interest in you won't last very long. Within twenty-four hours, if I have my way in the matter, you won't be worth twopence to them. Nor will George here, thank goodness. . . . Sandy, you must get yourself gaoled. The constable in Drumtoul—isn't his name Carfrae?—was telling me only the other day that they've built him a grand new lock-up at the bottom of his garden."

George, who had been listening to all this attentively, interrupted. "And what put it into a policeman's head to tell you that?"

"He was having a little joke." Cranston grinned at her. "About salmon. . . . And, Sandy—that will do for you. You must get Carfrae to clap you in his grand new lock-up for poaching salmon. You'll be safe enough there."

"Me jailed?" Sandy was indignant. "And with sic a record wad they ever promote me tae that——"

"Unjust suspicion, Sandy. Carfrae must let you out tomorrow evening, without troubling a magistrate. He can give you a note to your Superintendent. Or you can get your mother to write in that you were poorish."

Sandy took a hand from the wheel to scratch his head. This fertility in expedients was plainly something he remembered from of old. "It maun be as ye will," he said resignedly. "But will the tank laddies no' think it strange tae see three folk get oot o' an ambulance and gae louping ower the heather?"

"Not a bit. We'll look just like walkers you've given a lift to. . . . And you can stop any time now."

"Verra weel." Sandy hesitated and gave a sly glance at his former schoolfellow. "Might it no' be better," he asked, "if Miss Cranston here came tae Carfrae's new jile too?"

"It would wreck your chances at once." Cranston was decisive. "Carfrae's a decent shameful loon, Sandy, that would panic at the thought of it."

"He's got his auld auntie." Sandy held out this prospect of chaperonage without conviction.

"Stop havering, man—and signal them you're going to stop. I'll nip round behind and get out Day and the ruck-sack in no time."

Sandy Morrison did as he was bid. "D'ye ken what I think?" he asked. "That Day, whatever he hauds himsel' oot for, is but a coarse creature and no' worth a' this stour."

CHAPTER XII

CRANSTON HAD been prepared for difficulty, but their progress across the moor was even slower than he had feared. Day's eyes, although horribly inflamed, were beginning to be of some use to him—but they were no help with the heather at his feet. It looked as if the ten miles—and it was certainly a good ten miles to Urquhart—might take them four hours to cover.

For some time they had moved silently. The road had dropped out of sight behind them and the rumble of the tank column had died away. The only sound was the cry of peewits high in air, and sometimes a faint tinkle of water dropping in tiny invisible runlets down the slope they were painfully climbing. Helping Day was laborious, and after no more than half-an-hour they were glad to pause for breath. George had brought Sandy's binoculars, and she turned to sweep with them the ground over which they had come. The road, although below them, was still invisible behind some swell of the moor, and beyond it the heather stretched in reaches of dull purple to the sea. Nothing moved. In the whole prospect there was no hint of habitation. There was nowhere—whether in hut or tree or post—a single perpendicular line. Cranston, although he loved it, was prompted to apologise for the scene. "It's pretty bleak, isn't it? Vast and empty and useless."

"Vast?" George was amused. "If you came from Australia, you'd feel that this was no more than elbow-room."

Day had sat down, his head sunk between his hands.

Now he raised it. "Australia—is that where you come from? I nearly went there once."

"Really?" George looked at him coldly, and Cranston realised that she was unable to see in this queer fugitive anything remotely resembling a figure of sympathy. "A great deal of it is very like this, you know. Almost nothing to destroy."

"To destroy?" For a moment he seemed not to understand. "You think of me as a destroyer?"

"I don't know that I do. Perhaps it wouldn't be fair. Say just chief technical adviser to the Death Wish."

Day shook his head. Cranston noticed—as he had noticed when the man first came out of the sea—what a fine head it was. "It's a matter, of course, of what we're urged to—and given funds to go after. But it might have been called creative, not destructive—the Australian idea. Getting at artesian water—enormously far down. Transforming a continent."

George was silent for a moment. "But you didn't go."

"There were difficulties." Day looked up sombrely. Dimly, it appeared, he could now distinguish them as figures. "Had we better be getting along?"

They moved forward. It was still heavy going—the more so because, as George had foretold, the day was indeed a cow. A light breeze that had been whispering in the dried bells of the old heather had now died away, and the warm dry scent came up to them in waves. They had made another mile before George spoke. "Is it like this all the way?"

"We finish on a road—if we think it safe." Cranston stopped and fished out the map. "Let's get it clear. The high-road runs parallel to the road to Drumtoul we were travelling on. The distance between the two roads is about eight miles across this moor. But after about six miles we begin to have Urquhart Forest on our right. We could take to it, if the worst came to the worst."

"As it very conceivably may." Day, unable to see the map, was looking up at the sky. "I don't deny that this is a good move of yours, Cranston. But it's one they may well take a guess at. *They* would see that *we* must see the danger of simply driving into Drumtoul."

"That's clear enough." George was impatient. "But would they reckon on our moving almost due north?"

"They'd consider it. But they certainly couldn't risk throwing all their force into quartering this moor." Day spoke slowly, as one carefully weighing chances. "They haven't got companies at their command—or even platoons—after all. Their best chance is with the roads. What are they like round here?" He tapped the map irritably. "I wish I could see that damned thing."

"Imagine two adjacent squares," Cranston said. "Imagine them lying almost north and south. The southernmost line is the sea—the Firth. The line which they have in common is the Drumtoul road. And the line to the north is the high-road."

"Which we have to cross?"

"We have to cross the high-road to get to Urquhart, which is two miles beyond. We're going to make the high-road, I hope, at a pub, the Canty Quean. And there we can leave the heather. Imagine an inverted T. The arms are the high-road. We go straight down the stem, which is a by-road leading to Urquhart."

"I see. Would it be right to say that, until we get over the arms of the T, we are on a rectangular of bare moor, bounded by straight and virtually unfrequented roads?"

"Yes—and we are on a line that pretty well bisects that rectangle now. And it's bare enough—except for the forest, which lies north-east of us."

Day nodded. "Their plan will be to contain us, won't it? It's not too difficult to keep an eye on long stretches of straight moorland road."

"Quite so." Cranston folded up the map and prepared to walk on. "That's why I want to cross the high-road by the Canty Quean. The woods come right up to it there, both on this and the Urquhart side. We can reconnoitre without being seen. . . . George, it's my turn with the rucksack.

She handed it over. "What about people at this pub?"

"There may be nobody more than the man and his wife. And after that I don't think there's a habitation until we drop into the clachan of Urquhart itself."

"The what?" George was at a loss.

"The village. It lies just south of the house."

Again they moved forward. It seemed to Cranston that Day was tiring. Perhaps it was the man's terrific swim beginning to tell. "If we just make the Canty Quean," he said, "—or the forest close by it—you can shelter, if you like, and I can go on. Lord Urquhart would send down a car."

Day shook his head. "I don't think I shall be beaten by a remaining six or seven miles. But aren't you rather confidently banking on the benevolent interest of this nobleman?"

Cranston laughed. "It's going to involve telling some lies. Do you mind?"

"Not if they are convincing lies, my dear young man."

"Well—I rather do mind, as a matter of fact." Cranston felt a now familiar irritation rising in him. "I rather like old Lord Urquhart."

"But I understood you to say that he was the deadly enemy of your good friends at the castle. Perhaps that's irrelevant?"

"It's not, I'm afraid." Cranston frowned. "It's what I'll have to exploit. And I'll have to exploit your eyes, damn them." He flushed. "I'm sorry."

"Not at all, not at all." Day was bland. "You interest me. Did the castle folk blind me in an access of hideous barbarity?"

"Something of the sort. You'll have to back up the story that——"

Cranston broke off. George had stopped dead. "Listen!" she said.

"I wondered when you'd hear it." Day was at his most detached. "An aeroplane, without a doubt."

The sound hung, minute after minute, in air. In volume it rose, dropped, rose again, and then once more dropped. The suggestion was unmistakable; it was of a machine lazily circling somewhere far to the south. George searched the horizon with the binoculars. "Nothing to be seen. And I hardly suppose——" She was silent for a moment. "But one does come to feel that anything's possible."

Cranston nodded, but without much appearance of worry. "That's true enough. And it may be worth while, as we get along, keeping an eye open for cover."

"Are we likely," Day asked, "to find any—short of that forest?"

"I don't know that we are. But my guess is that the thing's harmless. If it comes in sight, we'll think again."

"Wait." George had turned a little to the west. "There it is—just coming over the horizon. It must be flying quite low. And it's only a little one."

"The job scarcely requires a B.47." Day had one of his flashes of savagery. "A ditch would help."

"Unfortunately we've hardly time to dig one." George

got her own back with some energy. "There's just heather. Given a little time, you could do something quite effective with that. But it's not exactly stuff you can climb under. What about sitting down on it for a start? They say it's movement that's first spotted from the air."

"Then we'll sit down." Cranston was still easy. "It should pass straight over us."

They sat down. The plane was revealing itself as a small flimsy thing. But for the increasingly audible throb of the engine one might have taken it for a glider. "A sort of run-about," George said.

Cranston followed it with his eye. "It's going straight home."

"Home?" She was puzzled.

"Lunch-time." Cranston spoke confidently. "And I'm hungry myself. Let's get on."

"Wait." George pointed. "You're wrong—whatever you mean by home. It's started fooling around again."

This was true. The little plane had banked and begun its lazy circling. It dropped in a wide spiral and rose again. Its movement was entirely the movement of a mechanical thing. Nevertheless, the suggestion it conveyed was that of a hawk.

Cranston spoke abruptly. "We'll take no extra risks. Down on our tummies is the thing. Heads under heather —and feet too, if it can be managed. Then don't move. And don't look up."

They got down as he directed, and lay quite still. "What's odd," George said, "is that we can talk—or even sing. Do you still think it isn't the enemy?"

Cranston laughed. "I think it's somebody quite different—our prospective host."

"Whatever are you talking about?"

"Old Lord Urquhart. He's air crazy, and has a little

fleet of aircraft of his own. He's one of the Scottish Representative Peers——"

"What does that mean?"

"That he's in the House of Lords. And he's constantly making speeches there about opening up the Highlands by means of air transport. Most enterprising, too." Cranston raised his voice, for the sound of the engine was now rapidly increasing. "Last summer he sold a herd of Highland cattle to the Duke of Horton—and dropped them by parachute into the park at Scamnum Court. And he does a lot of flying himself. It's my guess that here he is, having a little morning spin."

"I hope you're right. And I hope it's cooler up there than it is grovelling like this. . . . Listen!"

What there was to listen to was sudden silence. It was a good deal more unnerving than the mounting roar of the engine had been. Then suddenly the heather was whipping and tossing around them, and for a fraction of a second they lay not in bright sunshine but in shadow. It passed over them like a blade and in the same instant the engine broke into life again. Cranston looked up. The little plane seemed to skim the heather straight in front of his nose. Then it climbed and vanished from his field of vision. He had caught a glimpse of the pilot, a white-helmeted figure in an open cockpit. He had a confused impression that the man had waved an arm.

For minutes they continued to lie still. But the sound of the engine now steadily receded, and as it died away they sat up. It was only a speck in the sky in front of them. It glinted momentarily in the sun and then vanished.

"I hope you were right." Day spoke rather grimly as they trudged on.

"It's in the direction of Urquhart, more or less, that it

has vanished." Cranston was still cheerful. "So I still think it's our eccentric peer. And I hope I'm right about his going home to lunch. If we don't find him about the place, we shall be badly held up."

George, who had retrieved the rucksack, hitched it higher on her shoulders. "Richard, what sort of a place is this Urquhart anyway? Is it grander than Dinwiddie Castle?"

"Good lord, yes. It's one of Scotland's best attempts at a great house."

Day had taken off the dark glasses and was cautiously dabbing at his eyes with a handkerchief. "And you really have the entrée, my dear young man, to its splendours? We shall try not to be visibly over-awed."

"I know Lord Urquhart quite well." Cranston was curt. "How are your eyes?"

"Call them five per cent—which is a good deal better then they were. But they get more deucedly painful as they insist on seeing a little. Your father with his bandages might have been not a bad idea. . . . Isn't there a breeze again?"

George stopped. She was excited. "There is. And it's because we're at the top. Richard, what a tremendous view!"

"I hope I may be told about it." Day was ironic. "But if this means that we're posturing happily on a sky-line, I suggest that we move down a little."

"Quite right." Cranston moved on, pointing ahead as he did so. "There's Urquhart Forest, George, in the distance on the right. You can just see the high-road running from the left and plunging into it."

"And just there I see smoke—blue smoke."

"Peat smoke. That's the Canty Quean. It's all a good deal farther than it looks. Nearly a couple of hours, I'd say. Now look a little to the left—at about ten o'clock from the edge of the forest and on the very horizon. Can you just see a pale streak? That's Urquhart. A tremendous Doric façade."

"We'll make it yet." George spoke with sober confidence. "And I think I can now take a guess at why it's so desirable. You're reckoning that Lord Urquhart, if properly approached, will——"

George paused, and Cranston nodded. "Yes . . . fly us out."

CHAPTER XIII

Day was suddenly in a fever. It was as if energy had poured back into him so abundantly that he was unable to use it with economy. Cranston realised that until this moment he had been accompanying a man without hope. When in the quarry he had told Day that they were beaten, it had been something which Day already believed. He had been carrying on not out of any substantial hope but as the consequence of a sheer effort of will. Now he had seen a real chance. Only a few miles away there was waiting something that could transform his situation. He was moving forward with complete concentration on the physical task of covering with all possible speed this uneven and impeded ground. He was treating the moor as he had treated the ocean not many hours before.

But it was still a slow progress. Sandy Morrison—if he had been sufficiently impressed to do as he was told—was by this time in Constable Carfrae's lock-up in Drumtoul. Lord Urquhart had landed and was addressing himself to his luncheon—with a copy of *The Aeroplane*, Cranston seemed to remember, propped up against a large kebbuck of cheese. Caryl Blair was very probably consulting his father about her sprained ankle—and perhaps asking more questions than she ought to about the movements of the doctor's son. Sally——

Cranston checked himself and carefully scanned the country ahead. "I think," he said presently, "that we had better bear to the right now and skirt the forest. When we come to the last stretch—I mean before the high-road and the Canty Quean—we ought to do it through the trees. It's bound to slow us down a lot, but we can afford to be prudent before the last lap."

"And on the other side of the high-road?" Sweat was trickling down Day's forehead. It was clear that he still found it difficult and almost useless to open his eyes. His face looked as if it had been brutally scrubbed with some abrasive substance.

"We can either chance it and walk straight along the road. Or we can do a sort of Red Indian approach through the trees."

"Pine trees, I suppose?"

"Almost entirely." Cranston turned to George. "Did you ever play hide-and-seek in a pine wood? It's rather fun. You don't make a sound, because the ground is thick with the fallen needles. But you can't just hide behind a tree. It doesn't often have sufficient girth. And there's hardly any undergrowth. You have to keep far enough away from the chap that's after you to be screened by a whole band of trunks. It's like a game in some enormous colonnade. . . . Do you notice how the smell of the forest is getting on top of the smell of the heather as we approach? Do you like it?"

George sniffed. "It's all right. But it's not my idea of what trees should smell like. Did you ever smell eucalypts?"

"Gum trees?" He smiled. "Only in a botanic garden. Is it something hard to do without?"

She nodded. "Impossible."

Cranston glanced at her curiously. It hadn't occurred to him that a sun-goddess could be home-sick. "We'll get into the trees just there," he said—and pointed ahead. "But have a go at the high-road with the glasses first."

George sat down and carefully focused the binoculars,

balancing bare elbows on bare knees. "There's no sign of life about the pub. What did you say it's called?"

"The Canty Quean. It means the cheerful girl."

"It doesn't look cheerful—only rather lonely and forlorn. I can't think where it gets its customers." George swept the binoculars to the left. "But wait a minute. Perhaps there are some approaching now. Can you see? A car—a large closed car—coming slowly along the highroad from the west."

"I can see. It probably hasn't any idea of stopping. But we'll approach with a good deal of caution if it does. And now we take to the woods."

And presently they were moving silently through the trees. It made, quite suddenly, another world. Day would no longer be guided. The going had ceased to be treacherous underfoot, and out of the sunlight he seemed to find himself among massively distinguishable shapes. He went forward groping and peering. The effect was of something curiously savage. It was possible to feel that he would have been more congruously dressed in skins than in Sir Alex Blair's eminently civilised clothes. And if his sight was virtually useless still, his other senses appeared to have gained an almost primitive acuteness. "Listen." He had stopped—and the word was uttered only in a whisper. "There's a noise—a queer whistle." He relaxed. "Are there telephone wires?"

Cranston thought for a moment. "I think so."

George nodded. "I know there are—along the highroad. I noticed the posts."

"Then it's only the wind in them." Day had a strained smile that showed ghastly on his injured face. "But there's another thing. Somebody's cooking."

Cranston sniffed, but was aware of nothing. "Picnickers? It's more likely to be the old wife in the pub.

146

not fifty yards away. But I don't think we'll linger to
see what she has in the pot. Let's trust Lord Urquhart to
put on a magnificent cold collation round about three
o'clock."

"Do I get in on that?" George presented this question
with some urgency. "Your mother's was a dinkum breakfast. But I'm beginning to feel——"

Cranston nodded. The sun in some mysterious way
manufactures its own fuel. But it would be only reasonable
to suppose that George required substantial stoking.
"You're a problem," he said. "But my idea is to treat
you as Lord Urquhart's problem, and not mine. I hope
that *noblesse oblige* will do the rest. . . . And now, if you
ask me, the critical moment comes. Once across the high-
road, and I think we've beaten them. Come along."

They advanced until they were once more looking out
into bright sunlight. They were here among larches, and
these, running right up to the yard of the Canty Quean,
cast perpendicular lines of shadow across its white-washed
walls. The outlines of the building were uncertain, and
from their vantage-point it had the appearance of some
shapeless fleecy creature slumbering behind enormous
bars. The only sounds at first were that of a turkey
gobbling and a few poultry scratching in dust. It was
possible that to the high-road the Canty Quean presented
an aspect more in keeping with its name. The back was
dismal.

Cranston put his mouth to Day's ear. "Stay where you
are. I'll move round a bit and see what's doing."

Day nodded. "Very well. But be careful. I thought I
heard voices. And hadn't we better go east for a little way
and cross the high-road where it's running through the
forest?"

"Perhaps so—but I'll spy out the land." There was a

147

low tumbledown wall round the yard, and Cranston began to skirt it. The turkey still gobbled and there was the smell of a pig. He found that George was by his side. "Hadn't you better stop with him?" he murmured.

She shook her head. "Let's leave him for a minute. With any luck he may vanish."

"Vanish?" he was alarmed.

"Magically, I mean. Perhaps he isn't true. I'm sure I hope so."

Cranston glanced at her oddly, but had no time to speak. For suddenly there were voices from the front of the building. They stood quite still, straining their ears.

"Gentry," George whispered. "Or is it what Sandy calls half-gentry? I wouldn't know. But I think they must be from that car." Without waiting for a reply she tiptoed away, and he saw that she was determined to have first peep. He let her go. For he knew by now that George, although physically overwhelming, had a very adequate command over her slightest movements. And within a minute she was back. "It is. An enormous vintage Daimler, I think. And it's stopped with its bonnet turned down the road to Urquhart. It looks as if it might belong to your old Lord Urquhart's grandmother."

"It may at least belong to one of his venerable friends. I wonder——" Cranston hesitated. "Could you see who'd got out?"

"No—but it sounds like an elderly man. And I think he's talking to the woman of the place—the pub-keeper's wife."

"Mrs. Brash, I think she's called. If this is somebody going to Urquhart, do you think we might bag a lift? Could there be any risk—after we've taken a better look? It would mean we had it in the bag. Let's go round."

She looked at him in surprise—perhaps guessing that he

had somehow become infected with Day's new impatience. Then she put her hand on his arm. "I'll go. A
lone girl's more appealing at a first shot. If he's nice I can
spin a yarn and fetch you both out. But I won't break
cover until I get a better look."

"George, no——"

She slipped away before he could say more. He had
been on the verge of going forward himself, and her action
was taken on the strength of some sharp instinct. She
rounded the corner of the yard and looked up the high-
road as it ran through the forest. For as far as she could
see, it was deserted. She looked across to the road that led,
as she knew, to Urquhart. The big car was still stationary
—but in shadow, so that she could not distinguish its
occupants. She took a few steps farther and peeped
cautiously round the corner of the building. The main
door was there, sheltered by a small porch. The elderly
man appeared just about to turn away from it, and his
voice now came to her clearly. It was a Scottish voice—
dry, cultivated and full of authority.

"Then good day to you, Mrs. Brash. If your son still
seeks the tenancy, send him to see my factor. And I'll
speak to Lord Urquhart this afternoon."

The elderly man turned away from the door with a nod.
George made up her mind, and stepped into the road.
The elderly man saw her at once, and took off his hat
politely as he turned away to his car. His glance had been
appraising, courteously brief, and carefully unsurprised
and unamused. She made up her mind that he was a
judge. "Excuse me," she said, "but can you tell me the
road to Urquhart?"

He raised a silver-topped walking-stick and pointed.
"Two miles ahead—and well worth seeing. You can't
miss it." He appeared about to walk on, when a further

thought struck him. "Would you by any chance care for a lift? And have you friends with you? I think there is room for two or three."

"Thank you very much. I——" George stopped. Her eye had gone past the elderly man to the front of the Canty Quean. It was as forlorn as the back. But for the noise of domestic animals, one would have taken it to be deserted. She glanced at the little porch and the door within it—and suddenly her heart pounded. A shaft of sunlight, creeping round from the south-west, was playing full upon a large cobweb that draped alike the handle and the jamb of the door. The thing was as good as a seal. The elderly man had been conversing with nothing but a surface of blank wood.

He was looking at her with a changed expression. But it was only for a split second that she distinguished it, for a sound behind her made her turn in a flash. The doors of the big car were open, and she had a glimpse of a figure disappearing behind a dyke. She shouted with all her might. "It's a trap!" Then she ran.

The elderly man attempted no pursuit of her. She had the impression that he had instantly turned away, shouting orders. She ran to retrace her steps to the point at which she had left Cranston. Then it came to her that this was to give too much away. She wheeled and ran for the other side of the building. The move was a bad one. Another man was coming head on at her, and she had a confused impression of being caught between high walls. The man held something in a raised arm. It was as if he was going to strike her down as he ran and then hurry on to other quarry. There was a door on her left. She had no time to turn a handle, but she lunged at it and it gave. She was inside and she banged it to. There was a bolt and she shot it. The door rattled briefly, furiously, and then she

150

heard the man hurry on. Despite the uproar outside, there was no sound inside the building. She appeared to be alone in the Canty Quean.

She saw in a swift glance that it was a miserable place; she was even conscious that it smelled dismally of stale beer and stale tobacco. She was in a low back passage, and she ran forward into a kitchen. There was somebody in the place after all. A bent old woman was standing by a stove, stirring at something in a frying-pan. George called out and the old woman turned round. She stared at George vacantly and without surprise. Then she turned back, muttering, to her cookery. There could be no help there, and George ran on. She found herself in some sort of tap-room or bar. It was deserted except for a black cat, asleep on top of a barrel. She looked quickly round. It was her idea to find a weapon. She had a dim notion, picked up from stories, that such places often, for some reason, kept a loaded shot-gun over a fire-place. But what her eye fell upon was a telephone.

For a moment she stared at it, stupid and incredulous. The notion that she could have any link with an outer world seemed quite unreal. Then she ran to it. The instrument was fixed to the wall. There was a handle to turn—rather as if one were going to crank up an ancient car. . . . But almost at once a soft Scottish voice spoke. "Number please?"

She found that her mind was a blank. And then she remembered. "I want the police-station, please. The police-station at Drumtoul."

CHAPTER XIV

GEORGE'S SHOUT had brought Cranston out on the highroad at the double. For the first time since that fatal moment on the beach beneath Dinwiddie, when John Day had risen from the waters to fasten mysteriously upon him like an incubus, his mind was free of any thought of the man from the sea. There was nothing in his head but the girl—whom he had unforgivably let push forward as she had done. He had no hope that her shout was a false alarm—George was too reliable for that—and not much that he could in any way redeem the situation. But he made his dash all the same. He was in time to see her disappear round the other side of the Canty Quean. Simultaneously he was aware of several figures moving on the road, and he heard a call which told him he had been spotted.

He turned and doubled round the building, expecting to meet George that way. But she had vanished. There was a wall in front of him, and she might have got on the farther side of that—in which case its shelter would take her right to the fringe of the trees. His best course was to bank on this, and himself beat a retreat. If they could all three reunite, then they might contrive to withdraw into the forest and find another plan. He heard more shouts as he ran—not random shouts, but the sharp calling out of one and another command. It seemed to him that they were in English. The impression—quite irrationally—angered him more than anything had done yet. He supposed that in addition to their own secret agents—who must at least be brave men—they hired anybody they

152

ould get. He hoped that it wouldn't be before one of the
hirelings that he would go down—if go down he must.
And things looked bleak. A trap like this would take some
escaping from. Once more he had been far too confident.
He remembered his conviction that the little aeroplane
had carried Lord Urquhart, and the recollection made
him grin wryly as he ran.

Day was before him. Day was standing with his back to
a slender larch and in an attitude that suggested desperate
defiance. His face beneath its injuries was pale and
blotched and his nostrils were quivering. The man did, at
least, intensely care. And whether it was for his queer
scheme of atonement, or for some cunningly concealed
design, or again for mere life—the little of life that remained to him anyway—seemed at the moment unimportant. He would fight. Blinded and with bare hands he
would yet fight. And Cranston felt once more the tug of
whatever it had been that had first drawn him to the man.
It was something very primitive and probably entirely
worthless. It shocked him now, even as he felt it. For he
ought still to have no other thought than for George.
"Where is she?" he called. "Where's the girl?"

"Ssh!" Day had gone rigid. Now he turned on him his
furious purblind face. "You fool—don't shout! What
have you done? Another bungle?"

"Just that." Cranston lowered his voice. He felt no
animosity. "But haven't you seen her?"

"Have I seen anything—except men as trees walking?"
Day's hiss was again savage. "Get me out of this!
Haven't you landed me in it?"

It seemed to Cranston that the man was cracking. His
fighting would be that of a cornered animal. His swift
brain would no longer be behind it. Cranston put out a
hand to him. "Take hold," he said. "I'll get you a

couple of hundred yards back into the forest, and then . must have another look for George. I don't believe she made the trees at all. Perhaps she got into the pub."

He led Day back as he had promised. The enemy, he guessed, were doing nothing precipitate. They would be stringing out along the high-road, and across the last stretch of the moor, preparatory to making a drive through this corner of the forest. They still couldn't be legion—it strained credulity that there could be more than, say, a dozen of them all told—and they would have to spread themselves out thin, while carefully maintaining contact all the while.

Once more the Canty Quean appeared through the last fringe of trees. This time he decided to skirt it on the west, for it was on that side that George had vanished. He rounded the building—and there she was. But it was only for a second. She had darted out of some side door and bolted straight for the high-road before he could give a call. He ran after her. He supposed that she had got her directions wrong, and he risked a shout. "George—it's this way!"

He was too late. George had vanished round the front of the building. He followed—so precipitately that he tripped on a loose cobble and lost ground. When he reached the high-road she was over it. Suddenly he saw that she knew where she was going, and he stopped. The nearest man was twenty yards up the road where it plunged into the forest. And straight in front was the big car, apparently empty. George was making a brilliant bid to capture the enemy's transport. The man up the road had seen her and was pounding back towards the pub. It was just possible that she would bring it off, all the same. But even as her hand was on the door-handle she was beaten. Dead in front of her a second man sprang p as if from nowhere. George saw her danger, dashed across the narrow side-road, and vanished into the trees. Both men were after her. Cranston saw what he must do. "Day," he shouted, "this way—quick!"

The trick worked. Even as Cranston bolted he saw both men turn and make for the pub. He had a good start, and was securely invisible among the trees before they could catch a glimpse of him.

George was over the high-road. Provided she tried no more tricks, she was tolerably safe in the northern part of the forest, for the enemy was unlikely to spare it much immediate attention while they knew that their true quarry was close at hand in the south. And now he had better find Day again, if that was possible. It would be rash to shout, or even to give a low call. He must simply find his bearings, and then push cautiously about. Day could not be more than a couple of hundred yards away now.

He came upon him quite suddenly, sitting with his back against a tree, but alert and listening. "It's me— Cranston." He dropped down beside Day. The man was evidently tiring, but he knew how to conserve his strength. "Listen. It's not too bad."

"And what about your colonial giant?" Day had recovered his poise, and his question sounded decently concerned. "Have we lost her?"

"Yes. But I think she's got away. And we can get away too. We have this whole forest, after all. And these people can't run their hue and cry indefinitely."

"They have pertinacity."

"No doubt. And these are lonely parts. But it's not Siberia, and there are limits to what they can get away with. All this land is Lord Urquhart's—and he's pretty strict and enormously wealthy. He has no end of keepers.

They'll be on top of this invasion in no time." Cranston
realised that he had taken up the role of encouraging an
exhausted man. "Even if there are a dozen of these chaps
—two dozen—we can extend them hopelessly. We
needn't turn back. We can move eastwards through
the forest, parallel to the high-road. And after a couple of
miles we can reconnoitre it again. With luck we can be
across it after all—and within an hour. After that,
Urquhart's no distance, and we'll put our first plan
through. You'll be air-borne, man, by tea-time. So come
along."

Day had listened in silence to the whispered words.
Now he was on his feet. "That damned swim," he murmured. "Astonishing that I could race you straight after
it, and feel like death now. But I can do another couple of
hours. Or six at a pinch." His laugh was low but harsh.
"Lead the way. I can make you out."

Cranston turned silently and moved off through the
trees. It came to him that whether he in his turn could
make Day out was an open question still.

Within five minutes he knew that he had been wildly
optimistic in speaking of reaching Urquhart by tea-time.
If they could have brought themselves to walk straight
forward, with no more deviation than was required in
order to thread their way among the trees, the estimate
would no doubt have been reasonable. But that was impossible—because foolishly rash. Anywhere on their left
the enemy might be infiltrating into the forest. Indeed,
they were bound to do so, since they could scarcely afford
merely to command the high-road and play a waiting
game. Some sort of driving or encircling movement was
essential if they were to succeed. At any moment one of
them might appear, working forward from the road.

Against this threat there was considerable advantage to be gained by studying the configuration of the trees so as to find a route affording a maximum of concealment. This made progress very slow—and also distance hard to calculate. Cranston aimed at getting at least two miles east of the Canty Quean before any attempt to break through to the north.

They made perhaps a little more than half that distance in an hour. He was beginning to think of risking a turn to the left when something pulled him up. Only a short distance ahead, and directly across their path if they went on, there lay what it first occurred to him to think of as a great bar of light. For a moment the effect was of an enormous searchlight trained upon the forest. And then he realised that the occasion of it was very simple. What lay ahead was clear sunshine. But it could not, he knew, be the eastern boundary of Urquhart Forest. That, at this point, could not be less than five miles away. "Wait," he said to Day, and went cautiously forward.

A great straight ride was here cut through the forest—whether as a fire-break or for the convenience of sportsmen, Cranston didn't know. But for one set of hunters its utility was obvious. He stood still, listening. The only sound was the cooing of pigeons, invisible in the tree-tops overhead. It was a peaceful sleepy sound that made him only more aware of his own strained nerves. He moved forward to the edge of the ride—once more it was a matter of nerve-racking, time-consuming caution—and found a couple of tree-trunks from between which he could make a survey with reasonable safety. The high-road was a quarter of a mile away, beyond a long straight fall of ground. He could distinguish a figure on it—immobile and looking down the ride. Still with steady precaution, he looked the other way. At about an equal distance up the ride there was another figure.

Cranston turned and walked back to Day. "About turn," he said briefly.

"We can't go on?"

"There's a straight swathe cut through the forest. They command it."

Day nodded. He seemed again to be the calm Day of the earlier stages of the adventure. "Which leaves?"

"A damned sight less room for manœuvre, one has to admit. A triangle, in fact, bounded by this ride, the open moor, and the high-road."

"Listen."

It was the sound of a motor-horn—particularly sepulchral in tone—that had caught Day's attention. "Something on the road," Cranston said. "Another proof that this isn't Siberia. If we risk getting right up to the edge we might be able to dash out and intercept something. There's military traffic, for one thing."

"We could do quite a lot with just one of those tanks." Day turned round on this note of grim pleasantry, prepared to follow Cranston's retreat. Then he swayed on his feet and abruptly sat down. "Damn," he said. "Give me just a couple of minutes. Damn, damn."

"Take a rest—and spare your breath." Cranston stood beside the exhausted man, frowning. The conviction was coming to him that it was the end of their tether. If the enemy really had a dozen men, seven or eight of them could effectively seal this corner of the forest. And the rest could beat through it at their leisure. He strained his ears, but heard nothing except the same motor-horn, grown fainter. Within the forest twenty men could be moving in perfect silence over the deep carpeting fallen from the pines. "We'll try." He spoke quietly but sharply in Day's

158

ear. "Get up. You can do it. You said you could. We'll make for the high-road—and either lurk for a passing car or try a straight dash. Lean on me, if it's any help."

Day rose. His swollen eyelids had closed and he appeared drowsy. But he staggered on. "This Lord Urquhart," he murmured presently. "Might he know me?"

For a moment Cranston thought that Day's mind was wandering. "Know you?"

"I know he's not another titled dabbler in physics, like our friend Blair. But my notoriety—and the photographs?"

"Time enough to worry about that if we ever make Urquhart. And your face is a bit of a mess, you know. I doubt if anybody would recognise you who wasn't on the look-out for you."

"It's really nasty?"

"It certainly looks uncommonly painful."

"Rather a shock for my poor wife?"

Cranston made no reply. There was something false in the question which queerly jarred on him. And he wanted absolute silence. They must now be very near the road. Once he thought he heard voices—quite far away. Round about—and apart from the laboured breathing of the man beside him—it was almost ominously soundless. It was a relief when, some minutes later, there were unquestionably voices. They were not near, but they were nearer. They were the voices of men calling to one another as they moved systematically through the trees. The outer guards were all posted. The drive had begun.

"Come on." Cranston quickened his pace, and tightened his grip on Day's arm. "It's now or never, if you ask me."

They hurried on. The voices had ceased and there was

the silence again. But there was something wrong with it. Something that was wrong with it hammered at Cranston's brain. Of course there were the peaceful sleepy pigeons— but their sound was so constant that it counted with the silence itself. . . . He stopped dead in his tracks. Hundreds of pigeons. Perhaps thousands of them. But among them—a pigeon that was no pigeon at all. . . .

He wondered if he could recall the knack of it. He pursed his lips. "*Coo-too!*"

"Coo-too!"

"*Coo-too!*"

"In heaven's name!" Day had swung round on him, bewildered and furious.

"Quiet." Cranston breathed the word. He was intently listening. "I can't be wrong," he whispered. "I can't be."

"Coo-too!"

"This way." He dragged Day forward. The voices made themselves heard again—very briefly, this time, but again from nearer at hand.

"*Coo-too!*"

"Coo-too!" The sound came from close to them. They advanced a few more paces. Cranston caught a glimpse of the road, and of a dark vehicle which had apparently been run a few yards off it into a small clearing. Then, immediately before them, a figure stepped from behind a tree—an extraordinary figure enveloped in black garments and wearing an ancient silk-hat.

"Quick, man—for mercy's sake!" The freckled and perspiring face of Sandy Morrison was in violent agitation beneath the hat. "They're a' roon' us in thae lairicks." He gestured at the larch trees. "An' patrolling the road as thick as polis on a Saturday night on Edinburgh's Royal Mile. I'm jist hoping they'll tak' it I've steppit amang the trees for the sake o' daecency. . . . Noo, come awa'."

Sandy made a dash towards the road and they followed. The vehicle was a hearse. Beside the driver's empty seat was another sombrely clothed and hatted figure, oddly immobile. Sandy flung open a door and seized this appearance unceremoniously by the neck. Within a second he had it in the shelter of the trees, and Cranston found himself staring in stupor at a tailor's dummy. Sandy was tearing off its coat. "Frae auld Munroe's shop," he said. "I thievit it, the Lord help me, frae the window and dressed it as ye see. Lord sakes, Dickie, ye muckle looster —get yoursel' into the thing. They'll be doon the road ony minute."

Cranston did as he was told. "But Day?"

"The coffin, ye puir croot!" Sandy was in a frenzy. "I've backit the hearse so it canna well be seen. Ye maun thrust in the coarse creature and doon wi' the lid. I've bored yin-twa holes—God forgi' me for an irreligious man —that he can breathe through in the bottom. Quick man! Then I'll come oot, looking as I should, and awa' we gae."

Within a minute this extraordinary programme had accomplished itself. As Cranston jumped in beside Sandy he had a glimpse of a man sweeping up on a bicycle. Sandy slipped into gear and the hearse moved decorously forward. "Ye needna' look ower reverent," Sandy whispered. "In the profession, ye keep that until ye see the mourners. But let the big lum hat come well down ower your e'en. Did the chiel Day mind the coffin?"

"I think he was a bit taken aback."

"He'd be mair taken aback by a lang way if thae gomerils got at him with their guns. What kind of a daft gallivanting is this, I ask ye, to be rampaging in the ancient an' godly kingdom o' Scotland?" Sandy accelerated. "Where are ye for?"

"Urquhart. It's the first road on the right."

"Is it indeed?" Sandy was contemptuous. "If I didna' ken these pairts weel, d'ye think ye'd be riding in your carriage at this moment, Dickie Cranston?"

"No, indeed, Sandy. But how——?"

"Get your heid doon, man. Here's more o' them."

Cranston glanced ahead. It was the big Daimler—drawn up at the side of the road as if for a picnic. A cloth had been laid, and there was a hamper apparently ready to be unpacked. The only person visible was an elderly man of distinguished appearance, in dark clothes and a black hat. He might, Cranston thought, have been an eminent Q.C. Somewhat surprisingly, he seemed to be occupying himself with a portable radio. But as the hearse approached he rose and strolled to the edge of the road. At the same moment another man, dressed like a chauffeur, appeared on the other side of the road, one hand deep in a pocket. Both men scrutinised the hearse. And then the eminent Q.C. respectfully took off his hat. The chauffeur, accepting the cue, saluted. The hearse was past them. The Canty Quean was in sight.

"But, Sandy—how did you do it?"

The hearse was trundling down the side-road to Urquhart. The surface was bad, for Lord Urquhart disapproved of useless expenditure on facilitating surface travel. The trip could not be very comfortable for Day, but they had agreed that it would be imprudent to resurrect him yet.

"Man—it wasna' me. It was the lassie."

"The lassie?" For a moment Cranston's mind was blank.

"The lassie frae Australia, ye gaup. She rang up the polis at Drumtoul—rang them up frae the Canty Quean—and persuaded that great sloupe Carfrae to let me oot.

162

And me jiled na' mair than twenty meenits. The puir traicle came for me tae the lock-up tae mak' sense o' it. So awa' I went to find the ambulance. And then I saw there was little sense in that, for they'd mind it at yince after a' that cookuddy in the quarry. So I got oot the hearse instead." Sandy Morrison paused mournfully. "It seems no' likely, Dick Cranston, that I'll ever hae the chaunce o' driving it again."

Cranston laughed. "That you will, Sandy. I'll speak to Lord Urquhart. Isn't his word law from here to Inverness?"

"Even wi 'the Superintendent?"

"He appoints the Superintendent—and the folk that superintend the Superintendent as well."

"Would that be so, now?" This was a new vista to Sandy, and he received it with gravity. "But here's the lodge. Had we no' better have oot the creature Day?"

Cranston thought for a moment. "No," he said. "Decidedly not. We'll drive up exactly as we are."

CHAPTER XV

"I wouldn't have believed it." Lord Urquhart flourished the knife with which he was dissecting a cold ham. "Not, that is to say, if I hadn't seen it with my own eyes." He turned to Lady Urquhart. "Might be something in a shocker—eh?"

Lady Urquhart, who was combing a Dandie Dinmont, shook her head. "No, Ian—not a Cocker. I never cared for their ears. But we might consider a Golden Retriever." Lady Urquhart was very deaf. She was also a woman of somewhat circumscribed interests.

"But deuced like Alex Blair. Mark you, I never speak ill of a neighbour." With great rapidity Lord Urquhart cut half a dozen slices from the ham. "And much less of a neighbour's wife. It's something I never knew good come of yet. The servants pick it up, you know, and pass it on to the tenantry. And that's not good for any of us. So I never do it. What was I saying? Ah, yes. Damned foolish of Blair to marry that bitch."

"A bitch?" Lady Urquhart was doubtful. "But don't you think Alice would prefer a dog? One has to be so careful, in a town."

"An eminent ichthyologist." He turned to Cranston. "I think that's what you say the fellow is?"

"Yes, sir."

"And name of Knight?"

"John Knight."

"Quite so. I've heard of him, of course. Positively an outrage. I'm uncommonly shocked."

"No, dear—certainly not docked." This time Lady Urquhart was decided. "I never approved of it. Of course it may be different with sheep. There, I would never interfere." She turned to Cranston. "Is your friend Mr. Knight interested in dogs?"

"I think he may know about Russian setters."

"How very interesting! But such troublesome dogs to groom. A woolly and matted coat."

"Now, why doesn't the fellow join us?" Lord Urquhart looked about him hospitably. "Why doesn't he come and get something to eat?"

Lady Urquhart nodded. "Yes, Ian—that's just what I was saying. In town, *not* a bitch."

"Knight's making a long-distance call, sir. I believe he's trying to make certain of the whereabouts of his wife."

"To be sure. The poor lady will be very much distressed. Sheer barbarity. To be quite frank, I never regarded Alex Blair as one of us. Not even before that shocking low marriage." Lord Urquhart looked at Cranston. "Know Lady Blair, my boy?"

"I've got to know her a little better, just lately." Cranston wondered if he looked a fool. It was positively odd, he found, to be speaking a fragment of the truth.

"Take my advice and keep clear. If you ask me, the whole household's a bit strange."

"All spaniels do." Lady Urquhart appeared to admit this with regret. "But it always means that something has been wrong with the diet. And much can be done by treating the skin at once."

"Lady Blair's girl, now—can you remember her name?"

Habituated to deceit, Cranston gave the impression of exercising his memory. "Sally Dalrymple."

"That's right. . . . Have some salad, my boy." For a few moments Lord Urquhart busied himself about the table. "Although who Dalrymple was, heaven alone knows. Certainly not one of the Dalrymples. Queer girl, too."

"Sally's quite sound." Cranston found that, most indiscreetly, he had spoken with sudden fierce conviction.

"A hound?" Lady Urquhart took up politely what she plainly regarded as an inept suggestion. "An otterhound would be a possibility. But they are undeniably quarrelsome, you know. And there's that oily underfur to consider. Definitely not a dog that is *ever* at home in a drawing-room. And poor Alice, I fear, is scarcely at home anywhere else. I always advised against a political marriage."

"Quite right—quite right." For the first time, Lord Urquhart arrived at some sort of cloudy contact with his wife. "The political people have gone to the devil. No enterprise. Won't look forward. Travel in stage-coaches, if they had a chance. Now, take my grandfather. He wouldn't let the old Caledonian Railway, you know, put a line across his estate. Suffered a lot of abuse as a result. Called a backwoodsman and a Stone Age Pict and things of that sort. But not a bit of it. What he had was prospectiveness, my boy. Knew that all that railroad stuff would be obsolete within his own son's lifetime. Dipt into the future, as Tennyson said. Saw the heavens filled with commerce. . . . .Have I told you my scheme for flying fresh herring from Cromarty to Chicago?" Lord Urquhart broke off reluctantly. "Ah—here's Knight.'

An ancient manservant had appeared at the door. His words were unexpected. "Miss Cranston, your ladyship."

"My cousin, Georgiana Cranston." As George made her necessarily somewhat surprising appearance, Cranston offered what explanation he could. She was safe and sound, and his relief was enormous. But he did a little wonder what the Urquharts would make of her, and how much it would be necessary to fit her into the extravagant yarn he had delivered himself of. "Georgiana lives in Australia."

"Australia? How very interesting!" Lady Urquhart received her new guest with cordiality. "You must tell me about the dingoes."

"Dingoes?" Lord Urquhart was puzzled. "Never heard of such a family in my life. You can't mean the Stillgoes, Anne—the people poor Kinross's daughter married into?"

"Of course not, Ian. Dingoes are dogs. But are they pariah dogs? Nobody appears to know."

"Oh—dogs." Lord Urquhart's interest evaporated. "Can I give you some ham? Did you come with the hearse?"

George accepted ham. "I walked—through the forest."

"Perfectly proper, perfectly proper. I've no doubt you took reasonable care. You don't carry matches?"

"Never." George shook her head as she munched. Being introduced into the presence of the ancient nobility of Scotland did not appear to induce in her any access of self-consciousness. "Just a map and a compass and some lollies."

"Some——?" Lord Urquhart was at a loss.

"Sweets—usually barley-sugar. That sees you through twenty-four hours easily, if you get lost in a mist."

"Perfectly true, perfectly true." Lord Urquhart was delighted. He turned to his wife. "You see how well informed and well conducted the younger people are, Anne? And then a fellow like Blair goes and behaves in this disgraceful way. Has a gun fired under the nose of an eminent scientist—more eminent by a long way than Blair himself is, I don't doubt—and virtually blinds him and then hounds him over a moor. Supposes that everyone interested in fish must be a poacher."

"Certainly not. A lurcher would be quite impossible, Ian. We might as well send a greyhound while we were about it."

"Keeps keepers that are no better than thugs. Young Cranston here actually has to smuggle the fellow away in a hearse. Think of it—an ichthyologist in a hearse! But I must remember to commend this young Sandy Morrison. Most resourceful. I'm minded to give him a job on my ground staff." Lord Urquhart looked at Cranston. "How would that be?"

"Capital, sir—although Sandy has rather looked forward to doing funerals all the time."

"Then why shouldn't he?" Lord Urquhart was suddenly inspired. "Why not get that line of business into the air? Tiresome things, funerals, among surface traffic. Do it by helicopter, eh? I must consult my nephew. My nephew Porp, you know. He's the great helicopter-wallah." Lord Urquhart turned to George. "What about Australia? Any room for air-funerals there?"

"Well, there's plenty of *room*."

"We must think of it. What does your father do—make paper-bags?" Lord Urquhart paused and then appeared to recognise this as a somewhat random question. "Just that I get some money, from time to time, from people who do that out there. Make them out of gum-trees, I'm told. Deuced odd trade."

"My father raises sheep."

"Does he, indeed?" Lord Urquhart was interested. "Graze many acres?"

"I'm afraid I can't say how many. It's rather a hard sum." George considered. "But it works out at just under eight hundred square miles."

"God bless my soul!" Lord Urquhart was impressed. "What breed does he go in for?"

"Merinoes, mostly."

"Capital, capital." Suddenly Lord Urquhart put down his carving-knife and looked at George with something like awe. "Not the Cranston Merino?"

"You're telling me. And aren't they beaut?" George was enthusiastic. She caught Cranston's eye, and seemed to be moved by it to a further exercise of her vernacular. "Dinkum," she said.

Lord Urquhart accepted it gravely. "Precisely, my dear. The only word for that astonishing sheep. But—let me see—how did we get to sheep from fish? Cranston, what about your fish man? Isn't he going to join us?"

"I think he will in a minute, sir. But he's in a good deal of pain. You saw his eyes. They're in a shocking mess."

"Bless my soul—why didn't I think of a doctor?" Lord Urquhart was contrite. "Could we get your father over?"

"I doubt whether he could come, sir, just at the moment. He's standing by for rather a difficult confinement."

"I see, I see." Lord Urquhart considered. "What about old Anderson, then? He's said to be not bad. Some of the tenants swear by him."

"Then perhaps we'd better have him sir, although he mayn't know a great deal about eyes. But one can't pick and choose at the back of beyond."

"Eh—what's that?" Lord Urquhart was instantly indignant.

"Sorry, sir—but you know what I mean. The Highlands are shockingly out of reach of the great medical centres. Sir Mungo Lockhart of Edinburgh would be the man. My father says he's one of the best oculists in the country. But there's no hope of making Edinburgh under seven or eight hours."

"Indeed?" Lord Urquhart had risen and was eyeing his young guest with unusual severity. "And just where is this Lockhart to be found in Edinburgh?"

"Moray Place."

"Very well. Do you know Turnhouse?"

"Is that some sort of little airfield?"

"It is an airfield." Lord Urquhart contrived to utter this through a sort of snort. "And how long, do you think, would it take some wretched taxi-cab to get from Turnhouse to Moray Place?"

"I'm afraid I've no idea. But my guess would be half-an-hour."

"Very well. Add an hour and a half to that—or two hours with the devil of a head-wind—and you've got the time in which I can deliver this Lockhart his patient."

Cranston looked at his host with every appearance of astonishment. "You mean, sir, that you'll fly him there?"

"I'll fly the lot of you." Lord Urquhart had taken to pacing up and down in high excitement. "Go and find him. Go and tell him about it. And then send a telegram to Lockhart. . . . Sir Mungo, did you say? He must be one of the Lockharts of Lee. Perfectly sound people. . . . Ah, here your fellow is."

Day was led in by Lord Urquhart's butler. He wore the dark glasses Sally had provided in the summer-house, and Cranston wondered whether he was really still as blind as he made out. His appearance in this fashion, guiding himself on the arm of a venerable family retainer, had for Cranston a displeasing effect of masquerade. But then the whole thing was that, and he himself was up to the neck in it. And he was suddenly abominably ashamed.

He was both ashamed and bewildered—bewildered that

the quality of his shame over this merely graceless aspect of his situation was indistinguishable from that which he had been experiencing at what he thought of as his betrayal of Sally in the horror of his affair with her mother. Only some hours ago he had been feeling that to be utter dishonour—and the feeling had landed him, as a species of penance, with this queer mission. He still felt it as that now. But he found that he was quite as ashamed of this present charade—which was a mere harmless vulgar deception—as he had been of fornication and adultery. And the unexpectedness of this worried him. He could have enjoyed playing all sorts of outrageous jokes on old Lord Urquhart, just as a year or two ago he could have enjoyed stealing his trout. But this was the wrong sort of joke. And he found that he greatly cared about being committed to it.

But the feeling only made him plunge the more resolutely now. In for a penny, in for a pound. "Lady Urquhart," he said, "this is my friend John Knight." He had to put some emphasis on the name. He was afraid that Day might have forgotten it. And, even as he spoke, he had a sudden absurd panic about something else. Again and again since this adventure began, it seemed to him, he had blundered through over-confidence. And perhaps he had done it once more. It was wildly unlikely that either of the Urquharts had ever set eyes on John Day, the eminent nuclear physicist. Even if they had, it was most improbable that they would recognise him now. But it was not merely John Day who had just come into the room. It was also a complete outfit of Sir Alex Blair's. What if Lord Urquhart was accustomed to cast a noticing and satirical eye at his detested neighbour's sartorial tastes? What if he now gave a cry of astonishment and indignation? Cranston had managed a harrowing account of his friend's brutal treatment at the hands of hirelings of the Laird of Dinwiddie. It would take some explaining if it appeared that his friend was dressed in the Laird's clothing now.

The fear was, of course, baseless. Day—or Knight—was civilly received and accommodated with whisky and cold ham. He was convincing enough in his rôle—remarkably so, considering that he had to pick up much of it as he went along—but at the same time he was to Cranston's eye discernibly ill at ease. And Cranston conjectured with astonishment that it was a species of social embarrassment that was at work. The man who had been so confident with Caryl Blair was uncertain with harmless old doggy Lady Urquhart. He must have had dealings, in his final years of importance in England, with all sorts of eminent and exalted persons. Yet he couldn't quite get the Urquharts right. Not that it mattered. They were accustomed to it. But it was queer that this inwardly driven and outwardly hunted man, with his *idée fixe* and his passions and his small span of years or months to live, should retain the slightest responsiveness to the notion of comparative social elevations. Surely Day——

Abruptly Cranston realised that he had got it all wrong. Day's trouble was not embarrassment but some sort of distraction. The man was failing to keep his attention civilly on what was being said—whether by Lady Urquhart on the subject of Skye Terriers or by her husband on the insufficiencies of the Ministry of Civil Aviation. Perhaps it was sheer fatigue. Perhaps it was pain. Or perhaps—Cranston suddenly found himself thinking—it was a trick. Perhaps it was some sort of trick within his own trick—a matter of Day going one better.

"Cranston tells me that the man we had better get you to is Lockhart in Edinburgh." Lord Urquhart had come back to his plan. "I have told him to send the fellow a wire, to make sure you don't miss him. Eyes, you know, are not things to take risks with. It would be a thousand pities, my dear Dr. Knight, if this deplorable incident were to cripple a career like yours. Dash it all, we can't—um—know too much about fish. All very well for old savages like myself to catch them and eat them and order plaster casts of the big ones. But science is another matter." Having delivered himself of this amiable generality, Lord Urquhart returned to business. "So I propose, as I was saying, to fly you to Edinburgh. . . . By the way, I hope you got through on the telephone to your wife?"

"Not actually to my wife, Lord Urquhart." Day passed a hand across his forehead. "I had, as a matter of fact, rather worrying news. It bothers me much more than this business of my eyes."

"My dear sir, I am sorry to hear it." Lord Urquhart was concerned and benevolent. "Not, I hope, sudden serious illness?"

"A street-accident. You must forgive me if I am rather upset, and inattentive to your great kindness. My wife is in one of the metropolitan hospitals. And it seems that she is on the danger list." Day paused. "If you will really have the extreme goodness to fly me to Edinburgh, I can possibly get a commercial plane from there, or at least catch the night train."

"There is not a moment to lose." Lord Urquhart strode to the side of the room and rang a bell. "I shall fly you straight in to Northolt myself."

"My dear Lord Urquhart!" Day appeared painfully agitated. "I really could not think of it."

"Nonsense, my dear sir. It is my pleasure." Lord Urquhart was courteously concerned to minimise the sense of obligation his offer must impose. "Cranston will tell you that this is my great interest. There ought to be nobody in a position like mine in this country who is not equipped, and willing, to do precisely this. We must come down at Turnhouse to refuel, but after that it will be only one hop. And at Northolt my town car will be waiting to take you straight to your wife, and to such treatment as you require yourself."

Lord Urquhart, flushed and triumphant, turned aside to give orders to a servant who had entered the room. Cranston looked cautiously at George. It was evident that she shared his discomfort before this mounting duplicity. But decidedly they were in for it now. And with luck this amiable peer would never know that his confidence had been abused. Not, that was to say, unless the enemy won out after all, and riddled the anxious husband with a burst of bullets. Or unless. . . . Cranston knew—indefinably but with increasing certainty—that there were other possibilities. For John Day continued to be an enigma. His story was plausible—even convincing. But it remained true that to stick to him was to make oneself a fellow-traveller into the unknown. It was possible——

Cranston's speculations got no further. Lord Urquhart had turned to his wife. "My dear," he said, "I find that I must fly our guests south. Expect me home to-morrow. And don't blame our friends if their leave-taking seems a little abrupt. I am hurrying them along. We must leave now."

Lady Urquhart had listened carefully—and now her face lit up. "Precisely!" she said. "It has been in my own mind all the time. Alice shall have a Chow."

CHAPTER XVI

THEY SKIMMED over Scotland. Lord Urquhart—Cranston had found with relief—admitted the company of some sort of technical assistant in aeronautics. These two sat in front, and the three passengers in a small compartment behind. But Day had once more dropped off to sleep, and Cranston and George talked. He told her now all that he knew about the man from the sea. He tried to make clearer —he scarcely knew whether it was to her or to himself—the impulse prompting him to see Day through. But George appeared not much disposed to any large analysis. She was looking ahead. "Let's accept this business of seeing his wife. Even if it's genuine I'm not clear that it's admirable. But we can't possibly pretend to judge it, so we must take it as read. The question is: what then?"

"Yes—I know."

"I suppose, by the way, that the business about a street-accident was a pure lie—something cooked up to prompt Lord Urquhart to take him all the way south?"

Cranston shook his head. "I haven't had a chance to ask him—and I'm not inclined to wake him up now. But I suppose it's almost certainly untrue."

"Did he really make a long-distance call from Urquhart?"

"I can't even tell you that. But I suppose so. It would be a pointless deception, surely, simply to say he had. He wasn't going to ring up his wife herself. That would spoil the surprise."

"I think it's horrible." George was suddenly emphatic. "His eye must be entirely on himself."

"You said we couldn't judge."

"All right. But what about this telephone-call?"

"It was to be a cautious enquiry, I gathered, made somewhere else, to find out if his wife was still where he left her."

George looked puzzled. "Isn't that precisely where he might expect *not* to find her? Didn't you say there were children—sons? Surely when a thing like that happens one makes what break one can?"

"I suppose one might be determined to face it out. The address is somewhere in Kensington, and it seems she has remained there. I suppose it's an anonymous sort of place. And it's where Day asks to be taken to for this horrible reunion."

George was silent. She had turned away to look down at the country beneath. Its character was changing. There was a town. The sight of it prompted George to another topic. "Richard, what happened to my rucksack?"

He stared. "I'm frightfully sorry. It simply got left behind during the chase. I can't even remember where. Is it a disaster?"

She laughed. "We'll do well if we get away with no worse disaster than that—although I did like that frock. Is Turnhouse any sort of fashionable resort?"

"I'd hardly suppose so."

"Or Northolt? I do cut a frightful figure."

Cranston was taken by surprise. He even felt some sort of sudden shyness. His respect for George was now very wholesome, but he had started by regarding her as a figure of fun. This sudden unselfconscious emergence in her of matter of purely feminine concern for a moment disconcerted him. "You'll be all right if it doesn't turn cold," he said—and glanced at her cautiously to see how she would take this determined masculine impercipience. "And I have an aunt in London. She could——"

"That's all right." George was clearly not enchanted with the prospect of being rescued by Cranston's aunt. "My own base is in London for the time being, you know. I'm sharing a flat with another girl. And I do possess a spare frock there."

"Then that's fine." He hesitated. "Are you thinking of stopping in this country long?"

"Oh, no." She was briskly decided. "I'll make that visit to your mother, if I'm still wanted. But soon after that I'll be off. I've a job at home, you know."

"With the Merinos?"

Instead of replying, George pointed. "Are we there? Is that Edinburgh Castle?"

"Stirling. But we shall be at Turnhouse in no time now. The old boy wasn't boasting about the turn of speed he can manage."

"Must he really take us all the way? Isn't it a bit steep? There must be ordinary passenger flights from this Turnhouse place?"

Cranston nodded. "There are. In fact, there's bound to be one out just about the time we get there. But I suppose Day is going to feel safer tucked up cosily in private."

"It seems to me that John Day has it all his own way. If you ask me, this doomed-to-die business has got us both down."

"Perhaps. But it's only fair to remember that it has got him down too. I think we can trust Day to die."

"Do we leave him to it?"

For a moment Cranston was silent, staring in sombre perplexity at the sleeping man. "I'm sure it's true—that part of his story. But I'm not clear about just when the thing is—well, scheduled. It would be irresponsible, wouldn't it, just to say good-bye to him at the moment of tipping him into the bosom of his family?"

177

"Decidedly."

"In fact, one must whistle up a policeman at just that point? I've absolutely not given any undertaking not to. But it seems pretty squalid, all the same." He looked at her anxiously—caught himself, indeed, so looking, and suddenly realised that he was in a sense handing over to her. "Or doesn't it?"

George seemed not immediately disposed to tackle the question head-on. "Perhaps he means to do away with himself. That must have occurred to you."

"Yes, it has. I can't imagine that the sort of disease one gets from a slip-up with his kind of stuff can be other than unspeakably horrible. Suicide must almost certainly be in his mind. But it seems a bit mean to hope that the poor devil will hang himself just in order to get me out of a hole. I should never be quite sure afterwards that I hadn't actually bought him the rope."

"You've certainly given him a lot already." George shot this at him. "I'm a crude self-confident colonial, as you've noticed. But *your* self-confidence—your awful cheek, Richard Cranston, positively takes my breath away."

"My cheek?" He was startled and disturbed.

"Taking on a thing like this by way of getting straight with yourself over some small hole-and-corner immorality. It's outrageous. My younger brother once nearly started a bush fire."

"I don't see——"

"He had been shockingly careless. And it was about the very worst thing that he could have done. *He* saw it, poor kid, as a crime, a sin. He came back to the homestead feeling like death. But do you know what I found him doing half an hour later? Juggling with Dad's billiard balls before a mirror and showing off to himself no end."

"And I'm like that?" Cranston was looking at her round-eyed.

"Exactly. Except that your billiard balls are fissionable."

Cranston was silent for some minutes. The Firth of Forth had begun to broaden out on their left. The first part of their flight was almost over. "I wasn't regardless," he said. "I did think of bringing in Sir Alex Blair. But I found I just couldn't."

"Because of something about Blair himself? Or because he stood for society, the law—that sort of thing?"

Cranston found himself bewildered. "I don't know," he said. "Although obviously I ought to." He seized on a clarifying idea. "If Blair stands for society, then there's something rotten in the state of Denmark."

"So instead of Sir Alex Blair you brought in his stepdaughter, who is unquestionably sound? At least I think you described her to Lord Urquhart that way?"

"It wasn't like that, George. I've told you how Sally was dragged in. It was absolutely rotten for her, and she was frightfully decent."

"You don't think she——" George checked herself. "Do you think the enemy can have another shot?"

He nodded seriously. "I think they can. The business of the hearse wouldn't baffle them for long, and they would see that the trail led to Urquhart. When they saw Lord Urquhart's plane take off they would feel decidedly interested. I don't suggest we're going to be shot down in the air—but it's not at all certain what may be waiting for us, whether here at Turnhouse or in London. Then again, there's Day's wife. It wouldn't be beyond their imagination to fancy that he might make for her. And he *is* making for her. They may be waiting on her doorstep for him. In other words, despite bringing off this rapid move south, we have quite a bit of thinking to do."

179

"And surely with Day in on it? Mightn't it be suggested to him that he could find a healthier place for his bit of theatre than the known home of his wife?" She pointed. "Isn't that the Forth Bridge?"

"Yes—and we're coming down."

The plane banked and turned. An airfield appeared and disappeared, to be replaced alarmingly by hurtling roofs and haystacks. There was the slightest of quivers beneath them. "Nicely done," George said.

"There's the plane for London—that Admiral." Cranston nodded at a farther corner of the airfield. He glanced at his watch. "Due out, I think, in about half an hour."

"It will beat us, won't it?"

"I've no idea. Presumably we'll be off again within ten minutes ourselves. But there'll be time to stretch our legs. This plane isn't really built for you and me."

"I'd say we'd stretched them quite substantially to-day already."

For a moment they found themselves contemplating each other's sprawled limbs with frank amusement and satisfaction. Then Lord Urquhart turned round and gave them a triumphant wave. "First stage," he said.

They got a cup of tea, and afterwards George wandered off by herself. The whole business of air-travel fascinated her almost as much as it did Lord Urquhart. The great Constellations were to her generation what the mail-steamers had been to her parents'—the magically punctual carpets that carried one home—always, in a sense, "home" whether one were travelling in the one direction or the other. And the small fry—the D.H. Drovers and the Doves —represented the means of fetching the doctor or dropping in on the neighbours. But on this occasion she had only an absent eye for the traffic of the place. It had become clear to her that there was a sense in which her cousin Richard

Cranston had been hypnotised by his man from the sea. Cunningly—she was sure it was that—John Day had touched off in him something that was not so much simply romantic as positively atavic—a touchy quirky sense of personal honour that she knew in Cranstons on the other side of the world as well. Her own father called it the pride of folk who fetch long pedigrees from small places. And she wondered if the day's events didn't show her as a little tarred with the same brush—as indeed it was only natural that she should be.

So far, they had been rescuing Day from the people to whom he had formerly, for one reason or another, sold himself. What if the situation suddenly and sharply changed, and they had to shelter him—positively and immediately, in some concrete situation—from the law of his own country? How far was her cousin prepared to carry this hazardous business of a private judgment on the thing? And how far was she?

George stopped to look at the Admiral that would presently be taking off for London. Was it possible that the law had already been invoked, and that interest in John Day had spread beyond the small band of secret agents who had made all the running so far? Was Richard perhaps too confident that——

She turned away, seeing that it was time to go back to Lord Urquhart's plane. She was walking rapidly when she happened to turn her glance on the main entrance to the air-field. It was like the crisis when she had first spied the tell-tale cobweb on the door of the Canty Quean. But it was, for the moment, a good deal more bewildering. There was no sense in it. There was no sense in it unless— George found that she had stopped dead in her tracks. She heard a faint hail and turned her head to see her cousin standing by their plane and waving to her. She hurried forward. By the time she reached him her mind was made up. "Richard," she said, "I'm not coming further."

"Not coming?" He spoke above the roar of the engine. The plane was ready to take off. He was astonished and dismayed. "Why ever not?"

"I can't tell you."

"George!" He made a movement towards her.

"I can't tell you—yet."

"You're not——?" He paused, confused.

"Do you think I would?" She flashed it at him. "Where can I contact you?"

He saw that she meant it. "At my aunt's. Malvern Court. It's a big block of flats off——"

"I know. And now—get in."

Cranston gave her a single long look and obeyed.

"I'll be seeing you," she said—and turned away.

He didn't see it, she said to herself. For a wonder he didn't see it. And it sticks out a mile. It would be quite noticeable if it were black or a sober grey. But as it is——

There was only a chauffeur left in the great yellow car. It was drawing away from the low building marked *Departures*. George remembered thankfully that she had a belt—like Day she had a belt—and that there was quite a lot of money in it. Until she knew what was happening she couldn't afford to let go. She wished she was less absurdly dressed. Probably she was as noticeable as the yellow Cadillac itself.

She glanced quickly at the nearest group of people, with a notion that she would find them staring, and instead found to her astonishment that they were dressed exactly like herself. She drew nearer. They were young men and women of about her own age, talking a foreign language. For a brief moment—such is the power of recent associa-

182

tions—she was suspicious and alarmed. Then she slipped into the middle of them. They were blonde, and most of them were enormous. She guessed that they were Norwegians or Swedes. Certainly they were perfect cover. She stood in the middle of them, amiably smiling, and knew that for the moment she had found a sort of cloak of invisibility.

Not that there was any reason to suppose that Sir Alex Blair would know her from Adam—or Eve. Whatever he was up to—and to discover that was decidedly the point—he was presumably without the advantage of any information derived from the late enemy. From his own lodge-keeper, Patullo, he might vaguely have heard of the incident of the mysterious housemaid—supposing Patullo had in fact noticed anything. But that was the nearest, surely, that he could be to any knowledge of her existence.

And correspondingly she didn't know him. Her mind worked largely in pictures, and she had indeed invented an Alex Blair. She had invented, for that matter—and with rather more particularity—an image that she called Sally Dalrymple. But neither of these inventions would much serve for the purpose of positive identification. . . . She glanced about the species of assembly hall in which she was standing. There was no great crowd—only, she guessed, the passengers going to London on the Admiral, and an answering group going the other way to Aberdeen. And in a moment this conjecture confirmed itself. With the usual ritual of disembodied voices and lines of coloured lights the Aberdeen contingent was shepherded away. But her Scandinavians were going south—which was so far, so good. And so was she—or ten to one she was. The odds were sufficient to justify her buying a ticket at once. Without much trepidation now, she broke cover to do so. Fortunately the plane wasn't booked out. She returned to her adopted companions. They received her without surprise, and one or two even appeared to murmur casual words. Presumably their travels were young and they were some of them unknown to one another.

She scanned the remaining people in the hall. None of them answered to anything she could conceive of as a retired scientist turned Scottish country gentleman. She abandoned the men and studied the women. And almost at once she knew she was looking at Sally Dalrymple. Richard's Sally, she said to herself. Richard's sound Sally.

She was easy on the eyes. George framed this vulgar description to herself with deliberate relish. A sweetly pretty girl. No—that wouldn't do. It wasn't at all fair. Sally Dalrymple was beautiful. She was beautiful and knew how to get herself up to match. But she had told tales.

George took a grip on herself. One wanted a clear head. And to say—or think—a thing like that was less fair still. If the girl had gone straight to her step-father with the story of John Day one couldn't honestly and faithfully say that she had done wrong. And the consequence wasn't any sort of hue and cry. Turnhouse wasn't swarming with officers from whatever was the Scottish equivalent of Scotland Yard. Sir Alex Blair had acted swiftly—but unobtrusively. If the term didn't quite fit his Cadillac, George couldn't blame him for that. Had it not attracted her attention when she was scanning Dinwiddie Castle that morning, its sweeping on to the airfield would have meant nothing to her now.

Again she hunted around—for she couldn't believe that Sally Dalrymple was here alone. Sir Alex must be somewhere about. Unless indeed—it struck her suddenly as a possibility—the girl's travelling south to catch a plane was

184

sheer coincidence. But something about the girl herself indefinably insisted that it wasn't so. She was not only what is called perfectly groomed; she was also perfectly self-possessed. But if you watched her face you saw that it was set and strained. She was here because of John Day.

And she was here because she could identify John Day. Even if only in an imperfect early morning light, she had seen him as he now was. The moment must come at which the girl would have to point and say *There!* It couldn't be something she was looking forward to, poor kid—and it explained the tension discernible in her now.

The disembodied voice was telling the London passengers to get ready. And still there was no sign of Sir Alex. How, George wondered, did the girl feel about Richard? There was no doubt about how Richard felt towards the girl. Or about the whole story. George looked at the story steadily —much as she had been looking at Sally. There was nothing easy on the eyes about it. Still, her mind didn't exactly reel before it. Apparently poor Richard's did. He felt——

She caught herself up. All that wasn't, at the moment, the point. It was the point that this man Blair had been told of young Richard Cranston's rash involvement with the returned John Day. And what he was now doing— surely the facts could bear no other interpretation—was acting quickly and quietly to relieve the youth of at least some part of the burden of his folly. Presumably Sir Alex didn't know about the behaviour—about what newspapers or lawyers called the misconduct—of his wife. He thought of Richard as his step-daughter's friend and the family doctor's son. He would do what he could to get the matter briskly settled and effectively hushed up.

The voice was speaking again. They were being exhorted to follow the blue light. George's Scandinavians shouldered their rucksacks and bundles. The other passengers picked up their hand-baggage. There was a general shuffle across the hall. And then she saw him.

Sir Alex Blair was as unmistakable as Sally Dalrymple had been. He was the only person in the place, George thought, who had Ruling Class written all over him. If there was anything unexpected about him it was perhaps that the writing was a shade too large. He certainly wasn't showy or obtrusive or arrogant. There was nothing about him that corresponded, so to speak, directly to the colour of his car. Still, what the car spoke in one language the man himself contrived somehow to speak in another. Perhaps, George told herself, it was all to the good. He looked the sort of man who would prize powerful friends and cherish influential contacts. If Richard were threatened with serious trouble—and he might well be—this was the man who would know just where to go and what to say. Like his step-daughter he was beautifully turned out—in admirable clothes that were just not quite new. He was extremely well preserved, but not offensively so. He would smell—very very faintly—of some superb shaving-soap.

George had not much time to remark that these observations and responses fell some way short of enthusiasm. For now they were in the open air and had been taken over by a young lady in uniform. George managed to get right at the tail of her large blonde companions and thus to have Sally Dalrymple immediately behind her. Sir Alex, she realised, had been in a little office, and as he advanced she saw out of the corner of her eye that he was carrying a telegram.

"Just in time." He voice—pleasant, confident and not exactly subdued—came to her clearly. "It ought to have been waiting for us, but it came in only thirty seconds ago. A near thing. I asked——"

A sudden roar of engines drowned what followed. The Aberdeen plane was off down its runway. When the noise faded the two people behind George had fallen silent. The little ragged procession was nearing its aircraft. Two or three rude persons, having a mind to some favourite seat, began a sort of modified jostling designed to get them to the front. The Scandinavians stood politely aside. George decided to do the same. Without assertiveness—one couldn't indeed quite see how it was done—Sir Alex was first aboard after all, with his step-daughter beside him. George glimpsing them together as they went past, had an odd sensation of hearing with her inner ear the voice of old Lord Urquhart, repeating something he had already said that afternoon. Then she was on board herself. She didn't want to sit down beside a conversable Swede, and she moved forward. When she found a seat it was directly in front of the pair from Dinwiddie.

They were still, as far as she could judge, silent. But the engines were now roaring, and in a minute they were moving forward. It was only when they had been airborne for some time that she felt at all confident of being able to catch even fragments of anything that was said. It was years since she had eavesdropped in a serious way. She settled down to it now.

"There are a great many difficulties, you know, still." It was Sir Alex's voice. But its quality had changed. The tone matched the words. It was worried and almost sombre. "The biggest is the mere uncertainty."

"Are you so uncertain?"

"We have this one specific indication. Day is making for his wife. But it may be all lies. Do you think young Cranston realises that?"

"I don't know. I suppose he would. Wouldn't he?" Sally Dalrymple's voice, although distinguishable only with difficulty, came to George as oddly uncomfortable and constrained. It was as if she found talking about Richard difficult. And that, George thought, might well be.

"I know precious little about him." Sir Alex sounded impatient. "I suppose he's a fool. Most young people are."

"Thank you!" Now Sally's voice seemed to tremble. It might almost have been with anger. George frowned. Probably the impression was no more than a trick of the queer acoustics of the hurtling cylinder in which they were seated.

"Now, don't go off into idiocy, Sally. And stick to the point. We have this one positive line. Marlow."

"Marlow?"

"Weren't you listening? That's what Mason's telegram said. For the last twelve months the wretched woman has been living in a cottage at Marlow. So if it's *not* lies——"

"Yes—I see." Sally's voice sank, and George could only just catch the words. They sounded desperate. "I don't think I can take it. Dick——"

Sir Alex said something that George didn't catch. Nor did she hear Sally Dalrymple's reply. She had an impression indeed that it was less an articulate response than a quickly drawn breath or a gasp. And then neither said anything at all. The young lady in uniform had put on a different jacket and was handing out cups of coffee and sandwiches. The sandwiches were so sharply triangular that they might have been the product of precision instruments normally concerned with turning out components for the aircraft itself. Perhaps the people behind were munching them. For their silence continued.

England, slightly tilting from time to time as if it floated on a gently heaving sea, drifted beneath them on a leisurely trip to the North Pole. The Scandinavians, tired of cricking their necks in order to contemplate its dull mottle, buried themselves in guide-books to Cambridge, Oxford, Stoke-upon-Trent and other serious places. George began to think that her eavesdropping was over. At least she already had plenty to think about.

But perhaps half an hour later something more was said. Indeed, the two must have been murmuring inaudibly together for some time, since what she now heard plainly hitched on to other words just spoken.

"And if it is?" Sally's question seemed to be at once sharp and weary. "If it's an utterly false cast, is there anything else you can try?"

"Certainly there is. I can think of a good many possibilities. Perhaps Day has deserted his recent friends simply because he has secured a promise of more advantageous employment elsewhere. And he'll have brought with him on paper everything he can't carry in his head."

"But, Alex, where else——"

"My dear girl, plenty of countries are anxious to start up on all that. For instance, some in South America."

"South America? I don't see how——"

"You have no idea what I'm talking about." He was impatient again. "You seldom have. It's one of the points in which I find you rather like your mother. But you may think comparisons are——"

George heard no more. Two Scandinavians across the gangway on her left hand had started a noisy argument. It was earnest and good-humoured and went on interminably. For a long time she sat very still. She found herself wondering why she felt chilly. These things were air-conditioned, surely. And the late-afternoon sunshine was beating in on her right cheek as she sat. She had a queer impulse to look at the people behind her. If she could see them again it might help her to make sense of what she had heard. But she could do nothing by just turning round. The seats were more than head-high. She would have to stand up and deliberately stare.

That would never do. For a time the impulse left her and she felt sleepy. It had been a tearing-around sort of day. She must really—at least for minutes or seconds—have dropped off, because presently she had the sensation of starting suddenly awake. And again she wanted to have a look.

She remembered—it was absurd to have forgotten it—that there was some sort of wash-place at the tail of the plane. She had only to stand up and make for that. But now, oddly, she was reluctant. She tried to interest herself in the argumentative Swedes. They had got out some coins and bank-notes. The whole dispute appeared to be about the mysteries of British currency. She wondered whether she should lean across and explain it to them. She could do it in French. But that was stupid. They mightn't know French, and almost certainly they had a lot of English. . . .

Abruptly George stood up, turned, and began to walk down the gangway. She looked straight at Sally Dalrymple—Richard's Sally—and Sir Alex Blair. It was only a fleeting glance, and now she was moving steadily on.

But she felt very cold indeed.

CHAPTER XVII

LORD URQUHART'S town car turned into the quiet Kensington square, glided smoothly and silently half-way round and stopped. Lord Urquhart's chauffeur got out and impassively opened the door. Lord Urquhart had said good-bye at the airport and left them to give their own directions. Rather like a man who is careful of the stabling of his horse, he had explained that he had immediate instructions to give about his machine. But his quick withdrawal had been a matter of delicate feeling. Cranston wondered whether the chauffeur, when orders had been telephoned to him from Scotland, had been told that his destination was one of the big London hospitals. If he had, he had shown no surprise at this different destination.

Still sitting in the car, John Day peered intently round the square. Cranston knew that his sight had been clearing steadily all through the afternoon. The effect he gave was myopic, but he was in no difficulty. "It seems all clear," he said.

Cranston agreed. He was experiencing a sense of mingled relief and anti-climax. The more he thought about this moment, the more he had been inclined to see it in terms of melodrama. The enemy agents had lost their quarry in Urquhart Forest. Their next move—unless they simply decided to give up—would be to man any point where he was likely to reappear. And they would be bound to think of his wife. That they did not know her whereabouts was most improbable. And if they could raise, within a matter of hours, a force of a dozen agents in a remote part of Scotland, it was very clear that they would have no difficulty in finding whatever they required in London.

"But it *would* seem all clear." Day's former ironical manner had returned. "They wouldn't, when you come to think of it, have a couple of machine-guns waiting on the pavement. What one likes about these London squares is the gardens in the middle. Trees and shrubs galore. You could hide a small army in them." For a moment he sat back in the big limousine. "And, of course, a lot can be done from windows, too."

"No doubt." Cranston spoke shortly. Day's were certainly pertinent observations, but there seemed nothing to be gained by not getting the thing over. The chauffeur, moreover, was listening to these remarks with a wooden expression which Cranston found embarrassing. Cranston had been remembering the bullets spraying about the beach at Dinwiddie. But although it was a recollection which he found thoroughly uncomfortable, it did not exclude from his consciousness the absurdly incongruous discomfort of talking and behaving incomprehensibly before this waiting man. "We must chance it," he said. "We'll get out."

"Are *you* getting out?" Day appeared surprised.

"Of course I am." Cranston stepped on the pavement. "Thank you very much," he said to the chauffeur. "We don't want you to wait."

"Very good, sir." The man was looking not at Cranston but at Day, who was now descending from the car. "Good afternoon, sir." He was about to close the door when he glanced inside and stopped. "Excuse me." He reached forward to a seat. "I think these are yours, sir?" What he had picked up was Sally Dalrymple's dark glasses. He was still looking at Day as he handed them over. Perhaps, Cranston thought, he was quartered from time to time at

Urquhart, and had on some occasion been more noticing than his employer of the neighbouring Sir Alex Blair's clothes. But this was unlikely. And now the man had climbed back into his seat. In a moment the car had drawn away from the kerb and was gone.

"Well—thank you very much." Day, standing on the pavement, had turned to Cranston as a man might do to a friend by whom he has been given a casual lift.

It was the moment, Cranston knew, for which he ought to have been better prepared. He glanced round the square, almost wishing for the missing melodrama. But there was no hint of it. Behind its high iron railings the garden in the centre appeared deserted. The score or so of cars parked round about were all empty. The dusty London summer light was draining away, and sucking the dusk down into the great grey tank of a square. A boy was delivering evening papers, and down a side street a woman with high heels returned from shopping—the superior sort of shopping that declares itself in cartons and band-boxes of modish design. There was no help in this commonplace scene. Cranston turned and looked at the doorway by which they stood. "It's here?" he asked. "Your . . . home?"

Day nodded. "The top flat."

"You're going to stay?"

"In a sense—yes."

The man was inscrutable. One could be certain of nothing except that some inflexible purpose drove him. "You want me to go?" Cranston asked.

"To go?" For a moment Day looked at him as at somebody he had forgotten about. "Well—yes. Don't think me ungrateful. But for the moment—decidedly yes. It's scarcely an occasion, is it, for outsiders?"

"I suppose not. Shall you be here if I come back to-morrow?"

"That's difficult to say." Day fell silent. It might have been because a policeman was going past with a heavy and unhurried tread. Or it might have been in calculation—only by this time, surely, all his calculating had been done. "That's difficult," he repeated. "But I think not."

"Why?" Cranston made the question a challenge.

Day slightly shook his head. It was like a gesture of embarrassment. "Look," he said, "need we end on any sort of dismal note? We've had rather a good show."

"I want you to tell me, please."

"It's the top flat—five storeys up. Don't ask how I propose to leave it. Say . . . just rather suddenly."

"You can't. It's abominable!" Cranston suddenly knew that he was revolted. "I can't criticise the act. I've no right to. But you should have done it at once—long before you got yourself on that ship and within hail of this country. Let alone within hail of this house! Go away. Go away, man, and drown yourself. Only, if your wife's here, spare her this vicious stunt. You once said you wondered if what you'd got in your head was crazy. Well, it is. I see it now as utterly that. I ought never to have brought you."

Day's reply to this was to walk up the short flight of steps to the door of the house. There was a row of bells, but the door was open upon a staircase leading to the flats above. He turned. "*If* my wife is here? You don't believe me? I think you never did."

"If your story's true, and if you mean to do as you say, I can't see that there's anything I can do." Looking up at Day from the pavement, Cranston was seeing him rather as he had done during their first exchange of words among the rocks at Dinwiddie. "I urge you to give up this plan. But I can't do more. . . . *Is* it true?"

"It is true." Day's inflamed eyes held his squarely. "I give you my word of honour as a gentleman."

"Very well." Cranston turned and walked away.

It seemed to him that he had walked for hours. It was dark by the time that he went into a café and ate something—something tasteless and lumpish, washed down with what was perhaps coffee. He went out and again walked about London. He hadn't solved his problem; he had simply dropped it. He saw that he must begin with what he really knew—with what he really knew about the man from the sea. But his mind, as it tried to face this, went off elsewhere. Sally looking down at him as he descended the cliff—looking at him as if she never expected to see him again, as if it was all hopeless, as if this was the end. . . . It meant something, he now knew, that he didn't understand. This enigma worried at his mind. But so did another—and perhaps more keenly. George hadn't walked out on him. He was certain of that. Almost the only thing he had to hold to was that she was stopping in. But then why——?

He drove his mind back to Day. He tried to imagine George walking beside him—here in the London dark—and giving him a line on Day. He tried this for a long time. The spectral colloquy seemed fruitless—but presently he noticed the direction he was now walking in. He was going back to Kensington.

He must begin with what he really knew about the man from the sea. And the area of certainty was quite small. When one's head was clear it could be surveyed at a glance. The man from the sea was John Day—a scientist deeply compromised and immensely dangerous. Cranston found that his pace had quickened. When he reached the square he walked to the house with certainty and mounted the steps. There was a little frame for a card beside each bell, and a light good enough for reading. He looked at the one on top. It was something that he might have done before, he thought. If it said *Day* then his mind could be a little at' rest, surely, about the man from the sea. If it didn't, he was little farther forward. The poor woman might well be prompted to live behind somebody else's name. . . . There was a printed card in the frame. *DAY*.

For a moment he stared at it fixedly. He heard his own breath going out in a gasp of relief. The business was over —or over so far as he was concerned. Up there the abominable *dénouement* had by this time accomplished itself. Day had made his submission, penance, apology—whatever he conceived it. By this time, perhaps, he was dead. It was to be supposed that he would have the decency to choose a window at the back. . . . Cranston turned, descended the steps and walked away. It wasn't for him, he supposed, to do anything about the poor devil's wife—or not now. He didn't even know how she would feel about it. Perhaps she was not altogether hating that it had happened that way. Perhaps she was proud, happy, exalted. Day in his action might have been absolutely right. Cranston quickened his pace. It was beyond his experience. He just couldn't know.

He had walked a hundred yards when he suddenly pulled up dead. They wouldn't, Day had said, have a couple of machine-guns waiting on the pavement. But didn't that mean that he had left Day—been obliged to leave him—just at the very most dangerous point of all? Would Day's late employers much consider the feeling, or for that matter the life, of his wife? Had the affair had—or was it even now still having—a *dénouement* quite other than he had lately been imagining?

Cranston turned and walked quickly back. He must know. Even if it was the end of him—and it might be—he must know. He stopped and stared again at the card. *DAY*. It looked, he now saw, oddly new. Perhaps the poor lady lived here no longer, and it was by some trick that Day had been persuaded she did. Perhaps the top flat had been empty—until hastily invaded and transformed into a trap this very afternoon. With his imagination racing and his heart pounding, Cranston walked into the house and hurried upstairs, taking the treads two at a time. There would be another bell at the top. He had only to ring it and he could hardly escape finding out the truth either way.

He reached the top landing without consciousness of physical effort. There was another bell—and another little frame also. But this frame was empty. He could only barely distinguish the fact, because the landing was poorly lit. He paused to let his eyes grow accustomed to the gloom. He thought he heard voices.

Cranston strained his ears. One got odd effects in flats, and these voices might really be coming up from somewhere down below. If not, he thought, he knew where he was. Because they were the voices of men—several men—and they all appeared to be talking together. He put his ear to the door, and at once he was certain that the sound came not from downstairs but from inside. Suddenly the voices were louder, as if some inner door had been opened. And now he could distinguish something of their quality. They were foreign voices.

Some instinct made him draw back. Almost in the same moment the door by which he had been crouching opened It opened precipitately and a man hurried out. He was thrusting a soft dark hat on his head, and the movement took him past Cranston unheeding. He ran downstairs. The door began to close, as if somebody was shoving it to with a foot from inside. The voices were still talking, and in some sort of mounting excitement. Cranston couldn't be said to have made up his mind. His body acted for him. He moved up to the door, shoved against it hard, and walked into the flat.

CHAPTER XVIII

HE WAS confronting a small dark man with frightened eyes. The man began stuttering and stammering in an unknown tongue. As a door-keeper he was distinctly not formidable, but Cranston didn't delude himself he would find only the same sort inside. He put a hand on the small man's neck, swept him without much gentleness against the wall, and walked on.

He was making, he supposed, a demonstration—showing his private little Cranston flag. Well, that was how he had begun, and it did seem up to him to carry it through. Once more he recalled the bullets spraying on the beach. And this time he remembered also the voices calling from the quarry. They had been particularly detestable. And presumably it was the same voices—or the same sort of voices —that now came to him from some farther room. Decidedly, Day's pursuers had won. Day must have known about just this risk. But he had gone ahead. Dead or alive, he was worth some sort of salute. . . . Cranston pushed open another door. "Good evening," he said.

There was sudden dead silence, and then a small startling crash as somebody knocked over what must have been a bottle or a glass. Day was in a corner, and four men appeared to have been sitting round him in a close circle. Now they had sprung up and turned upon Cranston, staring. Only Day made no move. Even his bloodshot eyes were motionless in a face that had gone like chalk.

One of the men threw a swift question at Cranston—but not in English. Then he turned and talked volubly to one of his companions. A third joined in. But the fourth was silent, and this drew Cranston's eyes to him. Like the other three he was dark, and in dress he was not much distinguished from them. But he was very different, all the same. It was difficult to tell why. Perhaps it was simply because he assumed he was. And now he spoke a single sharp word. There was immediate silence.

Cranston took advantage of it. "It's all right, Day. I've got things in hand." He spoke slowly and distinctly. Then he turned to the others. "I suppose," he said, "that your trade makes it necessary for you to understand English. So listen. You are in the heart of London, and your chances are even smaller than those of your friends in the Highlands. I think you'd better give over. These antics are fit only for a comic strip—a decadent, bourgeois comic strip. I don't know whether this is still Mrs. Day's flat. But I'm pretty sure it's not yours. Clear out."

At least they were startled. The fourth man glanced at Cranston for a moment and then looked at Day. It almost had the appearance of being interrogatively. "This is altogether unforeseen," he said in English. "And most awkward. I appear to have been badly served." He turned and spoke rapidly to his companions in his own language. Cranston didn't understand a word. And yet suddenly the language told him a great deal. It was, in a fashion, speaking to him. It couldn't be the language it ought to have been. It wasn't nearly remote enough. In fact, it was Latin, not Slavonic, and distinguishably first or second cousin to languages he knew.

He took another look about the room—and then turned to the corner in which, according to his first impression, Day had been surrounded by a threatening group. Beside Day he now saw a low table. It held a decanter, a syphon, glasses and an open box of cigars. Cranston, who had been without consciousness of fear, suddenly felt rather sick. He walked up to Day and just managed to speak to him steadily. "Your wife—does she live here?"

They looked at each other directly. A muscle quivered at the corner of Day's mouth, and then with an effort he seemed to turn his face to stone. "My wife? Certainly not." He spoke with his old irony. "You must have been misled by the little card downstairs. But that was provided by these gentlemen, you know—just in case you happened to take a look."

"Have you a wife?"

"Dear me, yes. She is said to be living at Marlow." He shook his head. "But I doubt whether she would care to see me again. I would certainly not be so inconsiderate as to intrude upon her."

"I see."

There was a long silence. Cranston found that he was hoping to feel in himself some flare of anger. But it didn't come. Only the sense—the acute physical sensation—of sickness increased. He was learning that betrayal is the worst thing of all.

The fourth man took a step forward. "There is a distressing side to this," he said. "But, sir, you must take a balanced view. Thanks to you—for I am sure it is largely your doing—our friend here has got safely through. And from this point we know how to look after him. He is enlisted once more under the banner of the free peoples."

With an enormous effort, Cranston gave some attention to the man thus orotundly addressing him. "Are you Spanish?" he asked.

"My culture is Spanish. Let that for the moment suffice."

"In fact you come from South America somewhere? And you're proposing to smuggle Day away in your own interests? He's been plotting this with you—for a long time, and under the noses of the people he's been working for? If he managed to get clear of them and make this rendezvous you'd pick him up and get him away?"

"I must dispute the terms in which you express the matter." The fourth man suddenly smiled charmingly. "May I offer you a whisky-and-soda? No? Then let me put it rather differently. Let me ask you to consider this matter from the point of view of a civilised man, unfettered by narrow nationalistic notions. Our friend here is in great difficulty. He has abjured the errors into which he had lately fallen. You agree?" The fourth man paused. He was clearly pleased with his own excellent English. "But his own country can scarcely welcome him, or at once reinstate him in his labours—labours, mark you, invaluable for the cause of the free world. There would be vulgar outcry at once. You follow me, Mr.——?"

"Cranston." It was Day who composedly supplied the name.

"Thank you. We see, then, that Mr. Day is obliged to seek asylum—would you agree that asylum is the word? —elsewhere. And my country is honoured to provide it."

"I see." Cranston felt horribly tired. The whole business appeared weary, stale, flat and unprofitable. He couldn't look at Day now. It would be like looking on the very face of treachery. . . . Yet underneath the numbness and shock his brain was working. "Oughtn't you," he said to the fourth man, "to have a little talk about this with our Foreign Secretary? And haven't you, in joining in personally like this, rather overreached yourself?" He pointed to the fourth man's silent companions. "It's all very well sending people of that sort along to play a hand like this. But weighing in yourself is another matter. As you said a few minutes ago, it's most awkward."

The fourth man took a second to turn this over. "May I ask," he said, "what you take me for?"

"I don't know your country. Perhaps it's a big one or perhaps it's a little one. In either case it may well stand high in the world's regard." Cranston paused. "But I should take you to be its Minister at the Court of St. James'—or its Ambassador, if it runs to one. As I say, you've been indiscreet."

"It is arguable, Mr. Cranston, that you have been guilty of some little indiscretion yourself." The voice of the fourth man had taken on a new edge. "Let it be granted that publicity in the present matter would not be welcome to me. But no more, surely, would it be to you. There is again the factor of vulgar outcry. For nearly twenty-four hours you have been sheltering Mr. Day from the law. An inhuman law, no doubt, which enlightened persons like ourselves must be anxious to mitigate. But there it is. Technically, Mr. Day is chargeable with some very serious offence—and you have known it ever since you identified him." Abruptly the voice of the fourth man changed once more. "My dear young man—had you and I not better come to an understanding?"

"Look at Day." Cranston now spoke with energy. "*I* don't want to—but do *you* look at him. You'll see he knows that that's no good." Cranston tilted his chin. "At least he knows *that*—that I won't just say thank you and walk out quietly, promising to keep mum. Do you know what he is wondering? He's wondering if you're up to the standard of his former friends—those that he's been plotting to swop for you. Are you tough enough? That's his question. He knows that his only hope is in screwing you to murder."

"There is something in that." As Day spoke he reached for the decanter. "Our young friend, who began so decidedly as a romantic, is developing a realistic temper very fast. Unfortunately he clings to certain ideals of conduct. He won't, in fact, let go." Day turned to the fourth man. "In other words, my dear Sagasta, the decision lies with you."

The man called Sagasta drummed with his fingers on the back of a chair. He didn't like it. He walked slowly across the room and back, frowning. Then he gave a sudden nod. One of his assistants stepped instantly to the door.

Day laughed softly. "That's a little better. It looks as if we may reach your friends at Porthkennack—is it?—after all. But you'll have to keep your nerve."

Sagasta liked this still less. He had turned very pale. Cranston decided that the game wasn't quite lost. "It will never do," he said. "Even if you brought it off, your Government would never support you in it. They may want a big man in his line, like Day here, very much. They may be prepared to put him right at the top of a whole big show—which is what it's now clear to me he's prepared to sell and re-sell himself for, poor devil. But your Government won't stand for a big risk. They have no stomach, you know, for that sort of thing. Why should they have? The blood of the hidalgos doesn't exactly run in them—does it? Merchants and shopkeepers. They'd let you down."

This was a bow drawn decidedly at a venture. Yet it discernibly went home. Sagasta produced a handkerchief and delicately mopped his forehead. "I will take my chance, Mr. Cranston. There needn't, I think, be much risk of unpleasant publicity. If we can smuggle Mr. Day out of England alive, we can smuggle you out—how should I put it?—in another state of being. And we needn't take you so far. Say, just a little beyond the Lizard."

Sagasta gave a nod at another of his assistants. The

man's hand went to a pocket. And at that moment an electric bell rang sharply somewhere in the flat.

Cranston sat down. He was uncertain whether he did so as a gesture or because he was doubtful about the state of his knees. He still didn't believe that he was frightened, but he felt physically fagged out. It was how the truth about John Day had taken him. His voice, however, was perfectly steady. "I imagine," he said, "that we are now to be joined by the police. Tiresome for you all. . . . Yes, there they are."

The ringing of the bell had been immediately succeeded by a formidable knocking on an outer door. Sagasta snapped out an order to one of the men, who made a dash from the room. It was as if they had recalled the unreliable character of their janitor. But it was too late. There was a sound of brief expostulation in the hall, and then a new figure walked into the room. It was not, however, a policeman. It was Sir Alex Blair.

"Sorry to make such a row." He advanced, genial and confident, and swept the company with a rapid glance. "Good evening, Dick, my boy. No—don't get up. A pretty pickle you've contrived, I must say. And we must sort it out, I suppose—we must sort it out." Sir Alex drew off a pair of gloves, tossed them on a table, and briskly rubbed one against the other the palms of two perfectly manicured hands. "And John Day? Well, well—what a lot you must have to tell us. And what a change good Scotch whisky must be." He turned to Sagasta. "Your Excellency has a reputation as a man of enterprise—but I hardly expected to find you here in person. These gentlemen—yes." He waved a contemptuous hand at Sagasta's assistants. "I happened to know they operate here. And I decided to drop in."

"I don't understand you. There is, I think, some misapprehension." Sagasta was plainly discomposed, and for the moment could only fall back on conventional phrases.

"A misapprehension? I'd say there have been a good many. We believed, my dear Day, that you were interested in your wife. And your late friends—shall we call them the Hyperboreans?—appear to have been banking on that too. Marlow is swarming with them. But I had a shrewd idea you were really minded to other company. And here you are."

Sagasta had taken his little turn up and down the room. "You have brought your police with you?" he asked.

"The police will appear when it is appropriate that they should do so." Sir Alex's manner had changed. He had become grave and weighty. "I admit that the matter has its complications, Sagasta. This young man has got himself most undesirably involved in an affair he has had no proper understanding of. You follow me?"

Sagasta slightly inclined his head. "Possibilities open out," he said smoothly.

"And *you* follow me?" Sir Alex looked hard at Cranston.

"I suppose so." Cranston was confused. He was aware that he had to get new bearings.

"Then I think you had better go." Sir Alex was kindly but curt. "No purpose will be served by your remaining."

"But, Sir Alex—are you here alone? These people are——" Cranston paused, doubtful whether he was talking sense. "It's decent of you to try to get me out. But I'd like to know——"

"You must know already." Sir Alex appeared to misinterpret the unfinished question. "Sally told me—almost at once. She's a good girl, and you mustn't blame her. It was the only reasonable thing to do."

Cranston was silent. Of course the man was right. He

himself ought to say something at once—something to the effect that he indeed didn't blame Sally. But he found it impossible. The silence became strained.

"It's true, you know, that you *haven't* properly understood what you were about." Sir Alex was still kindly. "It was no affair, believe me, for romantic scurrying over the heather. Your first duty was to the security of your country, my dear boy. Well, that aspect of the matter is all right now. You can leave it to me. Go straight home and forget it. Forget it *entirely*. Do you understand me?"

Cranston nodded. Confusedly, he thought he did understand. Sir Alex was stretching a point—was stretching a point pretty far—in order to disentangle him from his follies. It was, as he had said, decent of Sir Alex. And over the face of this benevolent intention there lay a hideous and humiliating irony. The man who was thus taking risks with his own reputation—for it must amount to that—was Caryl's husband. Treachery all round. That was what it came to. Himself treacherous to Sir Alex. Day treacherous to him . . . Yes, he had better clear out. Sir Alex's standing by him in this way was the only decent spot in the affair. He had better do what he was told.

And Cranston stood up and moved towards the door. Nobody else stirred or said a word. There was some sort of doubt in his mind, but he couldn't place it. Something rather unexpected was happening. Or rather the unexpectedness was in the fact that something wasn't happening. The South Americans, who had been preparing a few minutes before to cut his throat, were doing nothing. They were simply letting him go. They were letting Sir Alex have it all his own way. But the puzzle, if there was a puzzle, was no longer any business of his. He had been charitably dismissed from the horrible involvement, and he had better go.

He had reached the door when behind him he heard a queer sound. It was a short high hysterical laugh.

Cranston swung round and looked at Day. The face of the man from the sea was as it had been—frozen into stone. But it was from Day, he knew, that the sound had come. Day had cracked. He was in a state of tension that had suddenly become intolerable. And for a second he had lost control of himself and given that meaningless laugh. But it was meaningless only because Cranston couldn't understand it. And he *must* understand. He walked back to the centre of the room. "It won't do," he said.

They were almost random words—for his mind was merely groping. But they had the effect of bringing Sagasta into action again. Once more he motioned one of his assistants to the door. "No, indeed," he said. "It won't do. Blair, can't you see——?"

"Leave us!" Sir Alex had swung round upon Cranston with a new uncontrolled vehemence. "Do as I say. If you remain——"

"But he must remain." Sagasta was suddenly vehement too. "Don't you see that the risk's too great?"

"Be quiet, you fool!" Sir Alex had turned upon him in a fury.

But it was too late. Cranston felt that he was now probably as pale as Day. But at least knowledge had come to him. He turned to Sagasta. "The idea," he asked quietly, "is that you're all going to talk business? Sir Alex, having tumbled to your game, is going to get in on some neat three-cornered deal?"

Sagasta's reply, if he proposed to give one, was forestalled by Day. Once more he gave his crazy laugh. But this time there was triumph in it. "You see?" he asked. "The boy has some sort of brain. He knows. It's the end of him, I'm afraid. But at least he knows." He stood up and tapped his waist. "Do you know, Cranston, what I have here? Enough——"

"You'll regret this." Sir Alex had turned on him savagely.

"Blair knows, my dear young man, that I must be carrying the records of enough new physics to give him what he has always wanted: a reputation. With this"—and again he tapped the hidden belt—"he could enter the field again and be no end of a swell. And he's prepared to do a deal. I leave him the stuff, and am free to take myself off with my new friends here—to another hemisphere. Would you say the proposal was reasonable? Do you advise me to accept?"

Cranston took one look at Sir Alex. A second wasn't necessary. The thing was true. Here again was betrayal, treachery. Without even knowing that he was doing so, Sir Alex had paid him back.

"But can I trust him?" With his enflamed eyes Day gave Sir Alex a glance that was ironically appraising. "Or can *you* trust him?" He had turned to Sagasta. "You see, now, where we stand? It's not just a question of the young man. It's a question of our venturesome friend Blair as well. A little time ago you mentioned the police. Well, as you see, you can put them out of your head. Blair is here on his own. It is really very rash of him."

"Do you think I'd be fool enough to come here without taking precautions?" Sir Alex's tone was contemptuous. "You may as well know——" He broke off. "What's that?"

It was the electric bell once more. It rang once and then for seconds there was absolute silence. The small man with the frightened eyes hurried into the room and whispered to Sagasta. And Sagasta turned to Sir Alex. ' At least it's true that somebody knows you're here. You're being asked for now. Will it much advance matters to deny your presence? I think not." He gave a brief order to the small man, who left the room.

A moment later, Sally Dalrymple entered it.

Cranston sprang towards her. The place was a trap. It had closed on him. It had closed on the treacherous Sir Alex. And now it was closing on Sally. Her step-father had committed some horrible outrage in thus exposing her. For she could know nothing of the true state of affairs. She could have no other notion of it than he himself had had only a few minutes before: that Sir Alex's concern was to bring the adventure to an honourable close and extricate the young man who had so rashly got involved in it.

But it was Sally who must be extricated now. The only chance was to use his fists, a bottle, a chair—anything that came to hand—and fight a way out for her at once. A· he took his spring to her side their eyes met. And in the same moment she cried out.

"*Alex, quick! He's getting away!*"

She had queerly misinterpreted his movement. And he felt himself go numb. His eyes continued to hold hers, and in a blinding moment her features interpreted themselves. Mysteriously and utterly, she was committed—was allknowingly committed—to the other side. She was this against some smothered longing, some broken hope within herself. And this was why now, as before, she looked despair.

"Pull yourself together." Sir Alex had turned on her. "Why did you come up?"

"Because they're here." Now she seemed almost dazed. "Because it's all found out."

Sagasta gave a sharp exclamation. "Found out? It's the police?"

"Yes . . . I think so," She was almost incoherent now. "A chauffeur—Lord Urquhart's chauffeur——"

"*Quick!*" Day had sprung to his feet, and his ghastly eyes were blazing. "I wondered—but I couldn't remember. It was the way he looked at me when he handed me the glasses. . . . He recognised me. He used to drive for the Ministry." He whirled on Sagasta. "Is there a back way? If not, I'm trapped. And so are you."

One of Sagasta's assistants was flinging open a door at the back of the room. There was a moment of complete confusion. Cranston's mind seemed to swim in it and then rise clear. He knew what he must do. He must get Day. He took a step forward, and in the same moment was hit on the head from behind.

He was down on the floor—in darkness, but aware of running feet, banging doors. The blow had been a glancing one, and he was up again. There was blood in his eyes. But he saw that only Sir Alex and Sally were left in the room. He threw himself at the door which he had seen flung open. It was firmly closed—bolted, it seemed, on the other side. He guessed that at the back of the building there would be either another staircase or a fire-escape. The South Americans would have got Day away down that. But now there was no way through. His only chance was to leave as he had come.

Cranston ran from the room. He didn't give a glance at the two people left there. He dashed from the flat and pounded down the staircase. If the police had really arrived —and Sally had seemed uncertain—he must contact them instantly. If not——

Hurtling round a turn on the stairs, he pulled up just in time to avoid violent collision with somebody coming up nearly as fast.

"Richard!"

It was George.

CHAPTER XIX

THE GREAT moon had passed its zenith. Far below them on their right the soft contours of Dorset rose and fell beneath its pale diffused light like a sleeper breathing beneath an eiderdown. On their left the still Channel was all silvered. It might, Cranston thought, have been last night's sea. But it was a different sea. And a different man was looking at it.

"Won't there be an awful row?" George had turned curiously to Lord Urquhart. "I mean, has he any business to have it out?"

"Porp?" Lord Urquhart chuckled happily. "No business at all. And I've no doubt that a missing naval helicopter is a serious matter. Almost as serious as a missing nuclear physicist. . . . Isn't that what you said the fellow was?"

"Yes. John Day."

"To be sure—John Day." Lord Urquhart was not particularly impressed. It was the aeronautical aspect of the expedition that interested him. "But I wouldn't worry about my nephew. Believe me, Porp Urquhart has taken on odder jobs than this. He did work with submarine-borne aircraft, you know. That's how he came to be called Porp. Short for Porpoise, you see—short for Porpoise. And as for a row—well, I telephoned the First Lord. We were at school together. He'll see Porp through, if necessary, with the salt-water chaps."

"And Porp can really find it?"

"I'm sure he can. A wonderful navigator is Porp. I thought of him at once, as soon as you explained the job to me. We'll be there, believe me, in under an hour." Lord Urquhart yawned contentedly. "You young people mind if I take a nap? No doubt you've things to talk about."

Like the sea and land below, Lord Urquhart slumbered.

"I hope you didn't get that name wrong." George looked anxiously at Cranston. "I can't see that the circumstances can have been favourable for accurate reception."

"Porthkennack? I got it correctly, all right. And I don't believe that Day noticed he gave it away—or that the other folk did either. They were all a bit strained, I'd say."

"And you know it?"

"I've been there. I don't say I'd recognise it. But that's this Porp's job. It's an out-of-the way sort of cove, but I know that sea-going craft sometimes put in there." Cranston paused. "I still don't know how you did it. Or how you began to tumble to the sort of affair it was."

George made no immediate reply. A helicopter is noisy. One wants to talk only in bursts. But presently she said: "Shall I take the hard question first?"

"The hard one?"

"How I came to guess the sort of affair it was. Their talk—when I sat in front of them on the flight to London, I mean—was queer. It would have been hard to tell just why. But it wasn't, somehow, the talk of two people who were acting quite simply in the interest of their country and of a rash young friend. But there was something else." George stopped and looked out on the quiet land and the quiet sea. "We seem a long way from it all, here," she said.

"Go on." Cranston too was looking far out over the dim landscape.

"It wasn't quite the talk of a man and his step-daughter

214

either. And then I got up and took a look at them. They weren't aware of it. And I saw."

There was a long silence. "I don't know how it could have happened," Cranston said. His voice was husky.

"Things do happen."

"Yes."

"There is something powerful about Sir Alex. And he must have exploited some horrible underground current of feeling. You get that in families, sometimes."

"Yes." Suddenly Cranston remembered. "She said that she knew how I felt . . . that at least she knew how I felt." He shivered. "Lord Urquhart understood what he was talking about, I suppose, when he said something about Dinwiddie being all wrong. He told me to keep clear."

"So I felt I had a better idea how things stood." George pushed on more briskly. "Sir Alex Blair just couldn't be more—well, corrupt. And it might take him just as much one way as another. And then I began thinking about Day too. He had told you his wife lived in Kensington. But Sir Alex had got that telegram, saying she had lived for a year at Marlow. I was sure there was more to the discrepancy than just a mistake. Day was trying to reach some address in Kensington, but not to see his wife. He had told you a lie."

"Quite a lot of lies." Cranston looked at her wryly. "Lies and lies and lies."

"I wondered what I ought to do. I could either try to hang on to—to those people, or I could go to the police. I had that address of your aunt's, but I knew that—well, that all sorts of things might have happened before I contacted you that way. I decided I'd stick to the trail. It was an idiotic notion."

"Idiotic?"

"Try it, and you'll see. In books people jump into a taxi, yelling *Follow that car*. Well, there was a car—and it was another yellow car, which might have helped. It was waiting for them at Northolt, and of course they simply got in and drove off. They had vanished from the landscape before I found anything. All I could do was to have myself driven to Marlow, and hope for the best."

"And it was a wild-goose chase?"

"Completely. I just didn't see those people and their yellow car again. And no end of people called Day live in Marlow, as I discovered from the telephone book. I could hardly go round the lot, enquiring whether they were related to a disgraced scientist. There seemed nothing for it but the police." George paused. "But then I felt that going to the police would be giving in."

"You felt that?" He was astonished.

George smiled. "Isn't it something that runs in our family? Anyway, I thought I'd make one more push in the name of private enterprise. And I thought of Lord Urquhart. He had a town house. Probably he had gone there."

"I think it was a wonderful idea."

"It was frightful cheek. I was very nervous about how he'd take it. And when I found him, he was interviewing his chauffeur. You know what the man was telling him— that he had driven yourself and the man called Knight to an address in Kensington, not to a hospital; and that he was sure Knight wasn't Knight at all, but Day. He had driven Day about a lot during the war, and he was certain of him."

"And the old boy wasn't furious?"

"At first he wasn't too pleased." George glanced cautiously at Lord Urquhart, who continued in slumber. "But I talked to him. I said I didn't want to let you down

—because it isn't a good thing to do in families. He agreed. And in the end he consented to my coming to explore the address to which his chauffeur had driven you. He insisted only on two things. One was that he should come too. And the other was that he should bring along some important old crony of his who could, if necessary, call out the whole British Army in thirty seconds. You know the rest. The real crisis was just after I'd found you—persuading him to make this one final bid of our own. The crony didn't much approve. But then luckily Lord Urquhart thought of his nephew Porp, and the idea went to his head. So here we are."

"And I think we must be nearly there." Cranston was scanning the coast below. "We mustn't muck it. We just mustn't let these South Americans get Day away on whatever ship they have waiting."

"What happens if we do?"

"An emergency meeting of the Cabinet, I expect, and a decision whether to stop on the high seas a ship belonging to a friendly power. . . . It's a pity you dislike the Tower of London, George."

"The Tower?"

He grinned at her. "It's where you and I will be incarcerated before being shot."

"Oh, dear! And Lord Urquhart?"

"He and Sandy Morrison will both be put in Constable Carfrae's new lock-up. Fortunately they'll get along together very well."

"We'd better not muck it, all the same. You really think our chances are good?"

"They're certainly not bad."

"And we'll be first on the scene?"

"We're bound to be—unless they have some means of flying down too. And I doubt that. Their resources are probably not on the scale of our earlier enemy's. They will just have some craft waiting off Porthkennack—probably a regular cargo vessel which has been instructed to take on the job. And they're motoring Day down to it now."

George nodded. "Will the chief man—Sagasta—be with them?"

"Not on your life. He's back in his Legation or Embassy by this time, resolved to leave this sort of thing to underlings in future. He didn't really have what it takes. And I don't think his assistants will have it, either. They want Day, but it's my guess that they'll ditch him as soon as they're thoroughly scared. And that's what we're out to have a shot at."

"Yes." George was silent for a moment. "Are you sorry for him?"

"For Day? I think I am. He seems to have guessed so damned badly."

"He began doing that a long time ago. Shall we ever understand him?"

Cranston considered. "He's not a venal man in the common sense. He hasn't been after money or the other obvious bribes. But he's no sort of political animal either, I'd say. Essentially, he's a misfit—a pathological egoist and individualist caught up in an activity requiring vast co-operative effort. His *idée fixe* is to be all alone at the top. And if he made South America he might, I suppose, end his days as a little dictator in his own virgin field there."

"He'd be top of his form—but still no more than one of the back-room boys."

"Just that. With all his near-genius, he's not exactly a far-sighted man."

CHAPTER XX

THERE WAS a small beach set in a deep rocky cove. The
sea was empty, the night still, and the moon sinking towards the west. It was uncannily like—and unlike—the
night before.

The helicopter had taken off again. It was invisible but
they could faintly hear its engine in the distance. After
dropping them it had moved inland. If it could locate a
likely car on the road to Porthkennack there would be an
opportunity for a first stroke in the war of nerves.

In the warm night they sat side by side with their backs
against a rock. Sometimes they talked. But for the most
part they were straining their ears, waiting to catch a first
low throb from the sea. Cranston wished it was over. He
didn't think there was going to be any violence or danger
this time. But perhaps he ought not to have let George
come, all the same. Perhaps he ought to have insisted
on her staying in the machine with Lord Urquhart and his
nephew. But he didn't at all know, for that matter,
whether George would accept a word of command from
him. And there was much more about her that he didn't
know. . . . He realised that here was another reason why
he was wishing it was over. It was all part of something
that was dead to him. But there was a lot he wanted to
ask George. And tell George. He turned to her now and
was about to speak. But she had raised a hand. "Listen!"
she said.

There could be no doubt about it. For a moment it was
no more than a tremor; then it was as if the sea had somewhere begun to throb to a deep slow pulse; then the sound

became louder and more commonplace. "Something quite large," Cranston said.

The engines stopped as he spoke. They waited in a breathless silence, gazing out beyond the line of rock that formed the western arm of the cove. For a fraction of a second the dark rock appeared to change shape against the glimmer of the sea. Then they were seeing the bows of a steamer. It glided forward without a sound. Small waves began to break among the rocks, and the whole surface of the cove shimmered. The steamer was almost stationary. There was a splash and a brief rattle. George stood up. "Anchored," she said. "We can't—thank goodness— have made any mistake. But what about finding some cover?"

He nodded, and scrambled to his feet. George in moon-light was like a statue cut in some dark golden stone. "The rocks," he said. They moved into shelter. "I think I hear the helicopter—and something else as well."

"Yes—it's a car. And travelling fast. Can a helicopter drop down to pass the time of day—or night—with a car going at seventy?"

"I'm sure it can, with the redoubtable Porp in charge. . . . And there he is."

The helicopter had appeared low on their right. Like a vast lazy insect it drifted across the face of the moon, and for a moment they could see the tail-rotor spinning. Then it moved out across the cove.

"They've lowered a launch from the steamer." George pointed. "And I can hear the car on the road down to the beach."

Cranston nodded. "It's a well-synchronised rendezvous, isn't it? But they're just going to become aware of the unexpected factor."

The launch was in the water. They watched it begin to

cut across the cove on a straight course for the beach. Suddenly it swerved and its engine faltered. "It's happened." George's voice—and it was for the first time, Cranston reflected, in their acquaintance—trembled with excitement. "They've seen it. Porp's dipping on them. It's a nasty shock."

The launch recovered and drove for the beach. The helicopter continued across the cove. It was hovering, mast-high, above the steamer. The launch beached, and almost at the same moment the car appeared. It was a big saloon. It drove to the edge of the beach and stopped. A door was flung open and four men tumbled out. They could be seen at once looking up at the sky. There could be no doubt that they too had been made aware of the menacing presence moving in it. The open door was shut violently from within. The car backed, turned, and tore off through the night. The driver, at least, had had enough.

The four men were running for the launch. Cranston could see that Day was in front. From the launch itself a couple of men had landed and were standing knee-deep in the sea, holding on to the gunwales. They could hear voices now— voluble Latin voices—raised in fierce dispute. One of the men from the launch was pointing back at the steamer. The helicopter had circled it and was now rising. And as it rose a light began to flash from it. It appeared to be sending a signal far out to sea.

The voices at the edge of the cove rose higher. Anger and panic could be heard in them. And suddenly there was a shouted command, a scuffle, a cry of pain. The men clustered round the launch were clambering into it, and in a moment it was streaking back across the cove. But one figure remained—prone on the beach. It was all over. John Day had been betrayed.

The launch disappeared within the shadow of the steamer. They could hear the engines starting and the anchor being raised. Within what seemed less than a minute the steamer was gliding from the cove, desperately seeking the immunity of the high seas. The helicopter accompanied it—grimly speeding the departing guest. The noises of both craft faded on the night. The ripples subsided. The cove and the spreading moonlit waters beyond it were void and still.

Day had got on his feet. He was standing quite immobile with his back to them. He might have been a holiday-maker with a taste for nocturnal seascapes. He was still in Sir Alex Blair's expensive clothes. "Wait," Cranston said. He rose from the rocks and walked slowly across the beach.

He was within arm's length of Day before the man turned. Cranston looked at him. "It's me," he said. The words were as flat as he could make them. He didn't want to import an ounce of drama into this last scene.

"It's you." Day eyed him wearily for a moment, and then turned and walked away. He was making for the nearest rocks. Cranston followed him. Day chose a flat ledge with apparent care and sat down. "Well?" he said.

"The helicopter will land presently. We go back to London in that." Cranston spoke quietly, finally. "Lord Urquhart has a friend who will see that the right things are done."

"The right things? But of course." Day had his old ironical smile. "And I nearly brought it off."

"You nearly brought it off." Handsomely, Cranston acknowledged it. Compunction faintly stirred in him. "I suppose it mayn't be so bad. After all, you *have* . . . come back."

"So I have." Day was amused. "By the way, one thing was true."

222

"That you haven't long to live?" Cranston accepted it gravely. "I never doubted it. And I don't doubt it now." He hesitated. "I'd suppose there is more than one way that you might feel about it."

"So wise so young, they say. . . ." Again Day smiled. "You remember?"

"I remember."

"And our race?"

"Yes."

Day stood up slowly. He seemed prepared for indefinite talk. "It wasn't quite on fair terms, you know—last night. I'd just done that swim. I can do better now."

Even as he spoke, he flashed into motion. It was totally unexpected, and he was fifteen yards ahead before Cranston started. On the beach he gained another ten yards. He had certainly been a sprinter. He was in the water and swimming.

"Day—come back!" Cranston paused for the one shout, and then flung himself into the sea. But Day was too far ahead. Cranston swam for a long time, but he glimpsed him only once. Or he thought he glimpsed him. But what he saw might have been only a clot of seaweed floating out with the tide.

He was very tired when he reached shore—but at once he scaled the highest rock he could find. The surface of the cove, and of the sea beyond it, was a great still empty sheet under the moon. Even as he had come, the man from the sea had departed again. The waters from which he had risen had closed over his head for ever.

"Richard!"

It was George calling anxiously from the farther rocks. Cranston was very tired indeed. But he turned towards the voice and ran.

THE END